A BROOKHAVEN PARANORMAL COZY MYSTERY
BOOK 8

HIGH WIRE

S.E. BIGLOW

For information contact; www.sarah-biglow.com

Edited by Alecia Goodman, Under Wraps Publishing

Cover Design by: Deranged Doctor Design

Print ISBN: 978-1-955988-67-4

Published by S.E. Biglow: August 2025

10 9 8 7 6 5 4 3 2 1

SPECIAL THANKS

I would like to thank all of the wonderful backers who supported this series on Kickstarter and made these books possible.

I need to give an extra special shout out to Heiko Koenig, GhostCat, pjs, John Idler, Sandy K., Anonymous Reader, Monica Kim, Matthew Walker, Ayl, Elizabeth W., Stephen Ballentine, Tracy 'Rayon' Fretwell, Julie McAtee, Melissa Showers, Kim, Kathy, Will 'It Work' Dansicker, Lisa Spaulding, Karin Baxter, Melissa, M. Kramer, Alexandra Corrsin, Katie, maileguy, Louisa Kannberg, Rob Steinberger, Brian, Anna McCluskey, Vannessa, Bridgette M. Findley, Mary F. Tallini, Amy Gentilini, Rosa, Stephanie Thomas, Taylor Park, Toby Rodgers, David Blethen, Amelia Pluck and Bonniejean Boettcher,

1

Something electric was in the air of Brookhaven as summer heated up. The vendors along the boardwalk opened earlier and the townspeople rushed into the outdoors at a more frequent rate. It meant the ambient hustle and bustle along the main streets of town came alive nearly at sunrise. I let out a soft moan and rolled over in bed to find the other side vacant. I groped blindly with one hand for a moment until it landed on the pillow next to me. It was cool to the touch. Opening my eyes, the room I shared with Maggie when I stayed at her flat greeted me in the early morning light. Pushing myself upright, I rubbed the sleep from my eyes and studied the empty half of the bed. The blankets looked almost as if they'd been pulled up and tucked in.

Climbing from beneath the sheets, I made my way into the living room and kitchen area. The bathroom was occupied, and I picked up on the sound of water running through pipes. The door opened and my girlfriend poked her head out. "I didn't wake you up, did I?"

Small puffs of steam wafted past her face, making her normally rosy cheeks a deeper shade of pink that complimented her short red hair. I offered a sleepy smile. "No. I think it's just the usual summer noise. You'd think I'd be used to it by now."

"One day you will be," she promised, stepping out of the bathroom dressed in an oversized t-shirt. She crossed the short distance and pulled me into an embrace, kissing me on the lips. "You know, since you're up ... you could join me."

Heat crept up the nape of my neck. "Much as that sounds lovely, I probably ought to get ready for work. Sage won't mind if I'm there early. We've had a boom in business since the weather turned warmer."

She pouted at me. "Sure, you won't reconsider?"

I caught the longing in her expression with a tinge of unspoken flirtation. While it was true High Time had seen an uptick in business, I didn't technically have to be at work for another two hours. "A shower sounds nice," I relented and followed her into the bathroom.

Nearly an hour later, I stood in front of the mirror, wiping away the fog with the dry edge of my towel to get a good look at my reflection. Maggie sat on the lid of the toilet tugging on her socks. It all felt so mundane. Not a word I used to describe many parts of my life these days. After all, we were both witches and pretty bloody good ones at that. I owed her and Tania so much for their help honing my skills.

"You've gone all pensive," Maggie stated as she stood up.

"I guess I'm just reflecting on how far I've come since I moved here. So much in my life has a changed. I've grown and a lot of that is because of you."

"Well, I for one am grateful you decided to come on holiday to our little town two years ago. Even if our first meeting wasn't exactly the meet cute, I'd have envisioned."

"I don't know, I happened to think you were awfully cute at our first meeting," I teased.

For a moment, I expected Sam to pop in through the doorway wearing his finest sparkling get-up and take the mick out of me for being so cheesy. But he had boundaries and since I'd been staying at Maggie's more often, he hadn't come around as much. I didn't expect to be hit with a pang of sadness at the realization that as my relationship with Maggie progressed, the little oddities I'd become used to at Tania's B&B became less a central part of my day-to-day existence. I made a silent promise to spend a few nights back at the B&B soon. After all, I hated thinking of Tania alone there, even if she did have Sam and Beau for company.

"Come on. How about we stop by Ginny's for breakfast before work? I heard there's going to be some temporary entertainment coming through town for a few weeks and you know Ginny will have all the gossip."

I followed her out of the bathroom and stopped in the bedroom long enough to grab my purse and tame my curls into a knot at the nape of my neck. Satisfied I'd be presentable for work, we walked down the street to Ginny's. The lights were off inside, and the door remained locked when I tugged on the handle. Checking the time, I frowned.

"She's always open this early." Ginny's cafe was one of the only shops on Main Street to open by six.

Maggie stepped beside me, peering through the

darkened glass. "I'd say maybe she's sick, but I don't think that woman has been ill a day in her life. You're right, something feels off."

Footsteps pounded on the sidewalk behind us. I spun, hope rising in my chest that Ginny had just missed her alarm and was hurrying to open the place up now. Instead, Vinnie approached, dressed in his uniform. He saw us waiting, noted the darkened interior and stopped short.

"You wouldn't happen to know what's going on?" I gestured to the cafe. No doubt there would be other regulars on their way, unaware they were about to be disappointed.

"I'm sure she's just late," he answered, averting his gaze.

"Vinnie, come on. It's us. If there's something up, we should know. I'd like to think we're Ginny's friends."

Vinnie tugged on his collar. "You didn't hear this from me, but she and Rick got into it last night down at the station. She came by to drop off some permits for the show coming through town and he ... well, he kind of lost it."

"What is this show? I've heard some people mention something's coming to town, but no details," I prodded.

"It's a traveling circus. Well, carnival really. Games, and a show under the big top. Honestly, I had thought Rick would have been happy to bring in the extra revenue for the town. I tried to point out if it did well, we could bring on additional officers to the department."

It did seem that the crime rate in Brookhaven these days justified at least one additional officer besides Vinnie and Rick. But why would the normally stoic police chief lose his mind over some permits? There had to be more to the story.

"What did he say?" Maggie asked helpfully.

"Just that she should have brought them to him sooner. He had concerns about the carnival, its staff, and security. He might have used a few choice words that I'm not going to repeat here."

I shifted my purse to my other shoulder. "So, can he just not allow them to set up?"

Vinnie shook his head. "The town council voted to approve the permits. I mean, I suppose he could refuse to provide security, but they'd just appoint me to run things."

I could hear the tiny voice in my head that came out whenever a mystery started to bloom growing louder. It urged me to talk to Ginny and see what was really going on. There definitely had to be more to the story. Either Vinnie didn't know every-thing, or he felt he couldn't share it. But I'd like to think that Ginny would be more forthcoming. I turned to Maggie and nodded for her to follow me. "Let's go see if we can get something quick at Tania's. I'm sure Ginny will come along when she's ready."

Maggie offered Vinnie a brief wave as she followed me down Main Street. "What's going on in that head of yours, Darcy?"

"The whole story about the permits sounds suspicious. Like, sure Rick is a stickler for the rules, but I doubt he'd lose his cool over late-filed paperwork."

"And you think getting food at Tania's is going to help how?"

I glanced over my shoulder to make sure Vinnie was no longer in sight before I changed direction. We doubled back and walked around Main Street until we came to Ginny's house. I could see lights on the first floor and marched up to the front door with Maggie trailing behind me. I knocked and rang the bell.

Footsteps sounded from within the house and a moment later, Ginny appeared in the doorway. Her hair was down, and she looked paler than I'd ever seen her. "I'll be at the cafe in like twenty minutes to open," she said softly.

"That's not why we came by," I replied. "We heard you and Rick had an argument yesterday and we just wanted to make sure you're okay."

Ginny opened the door wide as if to grant us entry and I crossed the threshold. She led us into the kitchen where an empty tub of mint chocolate chip ice cream sat on the counter. A single spoon sat in the sink, but a bowl was consciously absent. I couldn't help but flash back to the magic we'd done in this same space over Halloween in a bid to free our loved ones from a spell gone awry.

"Considering Rick would never have breathed a word of that to anyone, I'm guessing you ran into Vinnie and charmed information out of him."

"Didn't take much charming. He's worried about the both of you," Maggie noted.

"What's really going on?" I prodded.

"I think I made a mistake. A big one. And I only just realized it and Rick got angry. Angrier than I've seen my brother in a long time."

"That doesn't sound like Rick," Maggie pointed out.

"You weren't around the last time one of these carnivals came through. I should have realized something was off with all the paperwork. The names were just a little too normal. Too, uh ... anonymous to be real. The logo was a little different, but I should have recognized it."

"Ginny, what are you saying?" I stepped closer.

"Is it not a real carnival?" Maggie pressed.

"Oh, it's real alright. But the last time it came through town it had a different name. But I looked the carnival up and there's all the same acts. And I didn't want to believe it, but the same man's running it, too."

"So, they changed the name. That's not technically illegal," I said. "Rick couldn't blame you for not realizing it was someone who'd come through before.

"No, you don't understand." She spun to press her hands against the counter, blocking our view of her face. Despite that I could still see the way her whole body shook as she tried to hold in her emotions. "You know Rick's secret," she said softly.

"I think the whole town does by now," I replied.

"But you don't know how it happened. Not the whole story."

"He was young. You said he was changed against his will," Maggie said gently.

"It happened at a carnival. We didn't realize it

was full of supernatural creatures. There was never any proof, but Rick was certain the ring master had facilitated the attack that turned him."

"And you think it's the same man now, come back to town." I couldn't hide the horror in my tone.

"The way Rick lost it when he saw the photo told me ... Yes, it is the same man. And I don't know what to do. We can't pull the permits. They're going to be arriving tonight and will run for two weeks."

I reached out and placed a hand on Ginny's shoulder. "None of it is your fault. I don't think he's mad at you. He's understandably and justifiably worried about the safety of the town and the people he cares about."

"I'm just worried he's going to do something stupid."

"So, let's figure out how we can help Rick and keep his emotions from getting the better of him," Maggie suggested curtly.

"We could just get him really stoned," I offered, only half-joking.

Ginny gave a soft laugh and brushed her hair out of her face. "The one time my brother tried an edible, he lost control of his ability to keep the kitty in check. And then, once he'd shifted, getting him to change back was maddening. He just wanted to lay about. A stoned cougar is not what we need running around town."

Having seen the chief in his shifted form, I could picture the large tawny cougar lounging about and begging for belly rubs. It was honestly a hilarious mental picture that I couldn't quite shake, despite the seriousness of the situation at hand. I couldn't help but smile. Also, I was curious to know how he'd been afflicted in the first place. I'd always assumed he had magic like Ginny did. But he'd never displayed it. And any time he'd been in a position to use his supernatural abilities, the magic had always been tied to the wild cat he shifted into. Had whatever he'd been subjected to have altered his connection to magic? I'd never brought it up with the man. It always seemed far too personal. While I'd come to respect him, and he'd learned to trust me, we weren't the sort of acquaintances that shared intimate details of our lives with one another.

"Yeah, I don't think that's going to be the way to go," Maggie agreed, pulling me out of my mental reverie.

"What about a vacation?" I proposed. "I mean, maybe there's somewhere he's always wanted to visit. We could send him on a nice holiday while the carnival's here. Didn't Vinnie say that the town council would just appoint him to run things if Rick weren't around?"

"He'd never abandon the town when he perceives there to be danger," Ginny replied. "Besides, he's not exactly the most adventurous soul. Even getting him to go to Boston is a chore. So, luring him away for the duration of the carnival is out of the question."

"Then we just make sure he's never alone around the performers or the ringmaster," I said. "I'm sure we can get Tania, Sam, and Vinnie to pitch in to make sure he behaves himself."

"Rick's going to hate the idea, but honestly, it's probably the best thing we've got," Ginny admitted. She tugged her hair into a bun at the back of her head, accentuating the sharp angles of her cheekbones. She looked much more like the formidable woman I'd first encountered when I arrived in town. "Now, which of you is telling him the good news that he's got a chaperone for the next fourteen days?"

2

Maggie and I exchanged bemused glances. "Shouldn't it come from you?" I suggested. "I mean, you know him best. You understand what the carnival means to him."

Ginny shook her head. "No. I bring it up and he's just going to bite my head off."

And he wouldn't with us?

"We could propose it to Vinnie," Maggie proffered.

"We don't want Rick to get mad at poor Vinnie," I reminded her. Knowing I was going to regret it, I slowly raised my hand into the air. "I guess I'll do it. But I need coffee and maybe something for a peace offering."

Ginny spun and offered me a small smirk. "I can help with the coffee part. Wait here."

I watched her disappear in the direction of the basement. I couldn't help but hide my curiosity as she vanished from view. The only thing I knew to be down there was a room with only one point of entry and chains that Rick had used in his early days to restrain himself while in his shifted form. As far as I knew, there was nothing else. I strained my hearing as I caught footsteps echoing on the stairs and Ginny reappeared holding a slightly dusty can of coffee.

"I got this on a trip to South America. I promised I'd only break it out for special occasions. Rick knows I don't use it for just anything. You bring him a cup of this, he'll know I'm sorry and maybe he won't snap at you."

"Oh, I meant I needed the coffee for me. I'm not going to talk with your brother without some fortification," I replied.

Ginny set the tin down on the counter and retrieved a small knife. "In that case, you're about to have the best cup of coffee in your life. You're welcome."

I turned to Maggie. "I need to swing by Tania's for that peace offering. Meet me at the station in half an hour."

"I'll be there with enough coffee to bolster all of us," she promised.

I patted Ginny's arm. "Your brother's going to forgive you. He knows you do everything possible to keep his secret and keep this town safe."

Ginny didn't take her eyes off measuring the grounds from the can and running it through the coffee maker. "I just hope things don't go completely off the rails. Rick usually doesn't hold grudges, but this is different. This is a wound I'm not sure he's ever going to fully heal from ... and I just went and poured salt into it."

I didn't know what else to say to assuage her guilt. I couldn't blame her feeling the way she did. She'd devoted so much of her life to keeping Rick's ability to change forms a secret. She was fiercely devoted to her brother and this town. Our initial interactions were proof that she was hesitant to let newcomers in without a thorough vetting. Maybe she was still shaken from the events of Halloween.

"You should get going," Maggie noted, urging me towards the front door.

I hurried outside and traced the path to the B&B. It felt like a small weight lifted off my shoulders as I walked up the front steps of the porch and pushed the front door inwards. It still felt like coming home.

In hindsight, I should have knocked, but I knew Tania had no other guests. Still, I didn't need to give my landlady a heart attack.

"Tania, you home?" I called as I made a beeline for the kitchen. I could smell something cooking and I eyed a pot simmering on the stove as I entered the kitchen.

"Well, look what the cat dragged in," Sam's voice called out in a sing-song tone from across the room. He hovered in the center of the kitchen table, his torso bobbing in a macabre display, as if someone had cut him in half where he stood.

"Funny choice of words," I said softly.

That caught his attention, and he floated free of the table to bob at my eye level. I took in his vibrant red eye shadow and subtle blush to match a fiery red and orange sequined jacket with dark leather pants. It wasn't an outfit I'd seen him in before.

"What's got you so worried?" His lips turned into a pout.

"Darcy is that you?" Tania appeared from the living room, an empty coffee cup in her hand. "Oh, I wasn't expecting you today. Not that I'm complaining about seeing my favorite tenant."

"Uh, it's a bit of a complicated story," I began.

"Did Maggie kick you out? I'll haunt her pretty little butt for decades," Sam threatened.

"Sod off, you. No, nothing like that. It's just ... apparently the carnival coming to town has some history with Rick and Ginny is feeling guilty about bringing it here."

"What sort of history?" Tania set her cup in the sink and gestured for me to take a seat at the table.

"Ginny is pretty sure that even though the name is different, it's the same carnival where Rick was turned."

Tania let out a slow breath that turned into a sad sigh. "And since she's part of the town council, she feels responsible for not catching it."

"She's worried he might do something he'd regret. I sort of volunteered to stick with him while they're here just to make sure he doesn't go off the rails."

"You're a martyr," Sam said.

"I may have suggested you two might chip in, too. Just to keep an eye on him."

"My schedule's wide open," Tania said immediately.

Sam let out an annoyed huff. "I mean, I'm dead so what do I have going on. But it would have been nice for you not to assume I didn't have a busy social calendar."

"Thank you."

"What does Rick think of this arrangement?" Tania fixed me with an arched brow.

"He doesn't know yet. I came by to see if there was something you might be able to whip up as a peace offering when I go see him?"

"I think I can handle that." She rose from the table. "I made some Tres leches cake yesterday and I just happen to know he has a soft spot for it."

She pulled a dish from the fridge and doled out a serving into a travel container. "You are brave for offering to do this for Rick. I know how much this subject weighs on him."

I couldn't quite explain why I'd relented and offered to broach the topic with him. It wasn't like Rick and I were friends per se. But this part of him had always intrigued me and I wanted to know more about it, to connect with him over something magical. So, I accepted the container and made my way to the police station. Maggie waited for me with two of Ginny's large travel cups.

"None for you?" I did my best to balance the food and drinks.

"I had some before I left Ginny's. You want me in there with you?"

Yes!

"I can handle it."

"I'm only a phone call away if you need me. Text me to let me know how it goes, even if I'm on shift."

I nodded and pivoted on my heel. I needed to make this quick. My phone let out a loud beep reminding me that I only had half an hour until my shift at High Time and I didn't want to be late. I was grateful the doors to the station were automatic and slid open at my approach. I expected to see Vinnie inside, but he'd apparently gone looking elsewhere for breakfast. Or he was doing his best to avoid his boss until the whole thing had been smoothed over.

I could see the light on in the chief's office. I approached slowly, making sure to walk with deliberate steps, so that my feet echoed on the floor. I didn't need to spook the man. When I was about a half dozen paces from his door, I cleared my throat and called out, "Chief Hayes, are you in?"

Heavy footfalls sounded from within the office and Chief Hayes appeared. His usually neat uniform and hair were a bit disheveled, and I could see the hint of a five o'clock shadow that hadn't been shaved. His eyes were more amber than brown, and it unnerved me. He eyed the coffee cups and plastic container of food.

"Tell Ginny she can do her own damn dirty work."

"I'm not going to act like I fully understand what happened, but I do know that she's a wreck. She feels horrible for not realizing things about the carnival sooner." I took a tentative step closer and offered one of the cups. "She also told me that she got this brew in South America and keeps it for special occasions."

He warily accepted the cup, sniffed at it for a moment before taking a long drink. "She wasn't lying. It's good."

I took a dainty sip of mine and savored the rich flavor of the beans. I thought I tasted a hint of chocolate. Ginny knew her coffee. That was for sure. "I was hoping we could just talk for a minute?"

After a moment of indecision, followed by another long pull from the travel cup, he motioned for me to enter. I left the door open as I settled into one of the seats in front of his desk. He set his coffee down and smoothed his hair, rubbing at the stubble on his chin. "How much did Ginny tell you?'

"Just that what happened to you was associated

with a traveling carnival and that you think this is the same one."

"No, I know it is. I'll never forget that man's face. Ivan Gregor that smug prick. I swore I'd never let him set foot in my town again."

I noticed a flyer sitting on the edge of the chief's desk and picked it up. It was an advertisement for a traveling carnival that purported to have supernatural acts amongst its cast. Ran by a Silvan Church. The names didn't even sound similar. How could he believe they were the same? What had Ginny said again? She'd looked the guy up and he'd been the same man.

"Okay, so obviously we can't stop them from coming and putting on their show. Not without the town council getting more into your business than you want," I said.

"So, you've come with some sort of compromise?"

"We know that you're not going to abandon the town when there's a potential threat. So, let us help keep you grounded."

"Who is we exactly?"

"Well, me ... Maggie, Ginny, Vinnie, Tania, and Sam."

"Who's Sam?"

"Really?" I fixed him with an incredulous look. With everything we'd been through, I'd thought Sam had given up hiding around the lawman. Though I knew Sam could keep himself hidden, even from those with supernatural abilities if he didn't want to be spotted. "He's the ghost that haunts Tania's place. Cheeky bugger. Can't miss him in his rotating rainbow of sparkly jackets and tight leather trousers."

"I'll take your word for it."

"Anyway, it's just a precaution to make sure you don't do anything extralegal," I said, sounding hopeful.

I held out the container from Tania. "Also, Tania thought this might cheer you up."

Rick took the container, popped the lid off, and rummaged in his desk drawer for a fork. He dug in, not speaking, until the container was empty. The amber in his irises receded, leaning more to a natural human brown and even though he hadn't touched a razor, the stubble appeared less noticeable.

"Tell Tania I'll take her Tres leches cake any time." He set the fork down and looked at me. "You know they're going to be here for two weeks."

"I do. That's why we're going to rotate. You won't be alone with anyone from the carnival. We aren't going to let them re-traumatize you, Rick. You have my word."

"I'm not going to talk you out of this, am I?"

"Not a chance. I've said it before, and I meant it. You and this place are my family now. I want to see Brookhaven grow and flourish just as much as you. If that means we get a little closer over some candy floss and ring toss, so be it."

He wrinkled his nose at me, but broke out into a small smile. "As long as you don't expect me to win you a teddy bear or anything."

"Wouldn't dream of it. Besides, I think my girl-friend would be offended if you tried." I stood up as my phone buzzed in my pocket. "I need to head to work, but I'm happy to meet you wherever you need after my shift to welcome the carnival. Or whatever it is you have to do as a representative of local law enforcement."

"They'll be setting up on Tyson's property. Where we had the bonfire." He glanced away for a moment. "You remember where that is?"

"Funny enough, it's hard to forget where I came out to the entire town as a witch."

"Should be around four o'clock."

"See you then, Chief Hayes."

I took my still full cup of coffee and left the man sitting behind his desk. I downed the drink, which was somehow the perfect temperature in a few hasty pulls. I let the caffeine zip through my body, fortifying me for the day ahead.

BY THE TIME MY SHIFT ENDED, I WAS PRACTICALLY crawling out of my skin. All any of my co-workers could talk about was the carnival and the sales boost they hoped it would bring to High Time with the tourists. All I could envision was some shadowy stranger looming over the town.

Bidding the seedlings goodbye, I hurried through the break room, past the kitchen, and out to the employee lot of the dispensary. I was halfway up the street when I sensed a presence behind me. I did a quarter turn to reveal Sam hovering there.

"Don't lurk," I chided as I continued walking in the direction of the edge of town and Tyson's property.

"I assume we're babysitting the Kitty in Chief," Sam replied.

"You are bloody lucky you're already dead, because he'd kill you if he heard you call him that. But yes, he's agreed to have an escort accompany him around the carnival and its performers."

"Well, if anything, it'll be quite the show," Sam trilled and vanished, I assumed to fill in Maggie and Tania about the plan.

The sun sunk lower over the horizon as I approached the back of Tyson's Treasures, Brookhaven's only pawn shop. I spotted the proprietor, a tall, bald, dark-skinned man with a wiry frame gesturing towards a long row of vans at the far edge of the property. Rick stood in the shadow of the pawn shop, his uniform hat pulled down low over his face. I was halfway to him when a figure swooped in and intercepted me. He was a beefy man, with thick forearms, a bulbous nose, and slicked-back greying hair.

"Good afternoon, my dear," he greeted in a nasal tone. "Come to help set up?"

The way he leered at me turned my stomach and set my teeth on edge. I wouldn't have needed to see his picture anywhere before to surmise he was the ringmaster. "Just here to see a friend," I replied and gestured towards Rick who had left his seclusive post to make his way towards me.

"Ah, well, allow me to introduce myself." The man gave an overly dramatic bow. "Silvan Church, ringmaster extraordinaire."

How Rick hadn't already clobbered the man was beyond me. It was going to be a long two weeks.

In short order, Silvan turned back to the open space in front of us where people were darting around, erecting tall structures. I could almost picture the carnival rides emerging from the scaffolding before they materialized like magic. Out of the corner of my eye, I caught Rick staring daggers at Silvan. The flecks of amber in his eyes were shining brighter, his animal nature closer to the surface.

"So, how long have you run a traveling carnival?" I moved to physically put myself in Silvan's line of sight.

"Only a few years," he said. "I inherited it from a cousin upon his untimely demise."

"Oh, I'm sorry to hear that," I said, the words

tumbling past my lips on autopilot. If Rick was right, this man had no dearly departed cousin—untimely demise or otherwise—and yet his words had made me feel a sudden wave of sadness and sorrow for him anyway.

"When you're in this line of work, one's life expectancy drops. Dangerous stunts and all," he continued. "We've got the usual fun rides and silly games, but the real draw is the main show under the big top."

"I imagine it's got to be rather stressful taking over so suddenly," I prodded. "I don't know much about running this sort of business. But I assume there's a lot of paperwork, keeping track of everyone."

Silvan gave me a smile that looked almost predatory. "Really, keeping track of everyone isn't a problem, dear girl. We're a family, travel together and never leave until we've done a full headcount. Some of our acts have a tendency to wander off, but they don't' get far." He waggled his fingers as if to indicate he was casting some sort of magic.

Given that Rick had been turned into a cougar under this man's watch, I didn't doubt magic was around. Maybe that was what drew the carnival here in the first place. They could sense the power that coursed through Brookhaven's very essence. For a brief moment, I could see the carnival setting up shop in places like Boston or Salem, too.

"Have you done shows in every state?"

"The mainland forty-eight. Afraid it's a bit too chilly up in Alaska and not enough population to make it worth our while. And getting everyone to the islands is a bit ... precarious shall we say." He cast a furtive look at Rick, who'd resumed pacing a short distance from the back door of Tyson's shop.

"Can I ask what brought you here to Brookhaven?"

"The town's reputation, of course. It may have escaped your notice, I gather you're not from around here, but this little town isn't exactly as quaint as it might first appear."

The smarmy and condescending way he spoke made me bristle. Almost as if he thought only he knew Brookhaven's secrets. He was far more an outsider than I was at this point. I'd woven my story into the fabric of this town, and I found his assumption offensive. This must be how Ginny felt whenever anyone new came to town. And that brought up another question in the back of my mind. Why did Ginny agree to let them come through town in the first place? Had she really let the need for revenue and an infusion of tourism overshadow her protectiveness of the town and its residents?

"Oh, I'm quite familiar with the town's subtle appeal. Something tells me that you've got something similar going on here." I made a sweeping gesture at the rides erecting before our eyes and the enormous blue and white striped tent, its front flaps fluttering in the slight breeze.

"And what makes you think we're anything special?" Under Silvan's penetrating gaze I could feel words being pulled from deep within me. Things I didn't want to admit to this stranger.

"Because I recognize magic when I see it." It was as if the words burned my throat like bile.

"I thought so," he whispered in my ear.

My stomach churned as he continued to look at me, like an animal sizing up its prey. Before he could speak again, though, a woman in loose athletic pants and a mint green tank top came running over. "Silvan, we've got a situation. GhostCat's gone off the reservation again."

Silvan let out a disgusted sound. "It's just a cat. No need to worry your pretty head about it." When she didn't move, he let out another sigh and turned to look at me. "You'll have to forgive me."

I was relieved to be free of the man's presence as

he hurried off behind the woman. They disappeared into the tent, and I spun, looking for Rick. I found him standing dangerously close to the inner workings of what looked like a merry-go-round. The burly man who was fiddling with the mechanism looked less-than-happy to have an audience.

"Well, that man is nauseating," I announced to the chief when I was within earshot.

"Why do you think I stayed away from him?" Rick replied.

"I'll give it to you, you've got good self-control. Maybe this whole chaperone idea was a bit reactionary."

"If I'm honest, I was able to hold it together because you were the buffer," he admitted, moving away from the mechanic and around the other rides being completed and inspected.

"The man's got something like Ginny's magic. Like he could compel the truth out of me."

"I wouldn't say it's exactly like hers, but he's definitely got power and uses it to control people. I think it's how he keeps everyone here under his thumb."

"I know it's a sore subject, and it's really not my business, but he didn't look like he was capable of turning into a giant cat. So, how did he do it to you?"

Rick stiffened at my question, and I mentally

braced myself for him to become the man I'd first encountered on my arrival—distrustful, cut off. Instead, slowly, the tension melted from his shoulders. The vibrant shards of amber in his eyes receded until his irises were almost completely a normal human shade of brown.

"It's all a bit hazy, even now. But I know he lured me somewhere secluded. I knew I shouldn't have gone with him, but I couldn't help myself. It was as if my head was splitting open. It felt like my entire body was ripping itself apart. I've never felt so much pain. I'm fairly sure I blacked out at some point. But I remember his face looming over me with this look of expectation on it. And when I came to, he was gone. I could tell something was wrong with me, but I couldn't pinpoint what. Not until I changed the first time."

"That sounds horrible. Do you think he was hoping you'd join his carnival?"

Rick shook his head. "I don't know what went on in that sick bastard's mind. But I wasn't going to leave my family or this town. Even then I knew threats were out there like him, and I wasn't going to let them come through my town again."

"And that's why you ran for Chief of Police when you could." It came out as a statement rather than a question. I glanced over at the big top tent again and a shiver ran through me. I'd been in town nearly two years and had that time to wrap my head around magic. And it still amazed and surprised me.

"I know it probably doesn't mean a lot, but I think you've done a great job keeping your people safe." I held my tongue about the fact that there'd been a spike in murders and suspicious deaths since I'd set foot in town over the last two years. Mercifully, he didn't broach it either.

"I appreciate that."

"So, I know this all makes your skin crawl. But I assume you're out here for a reason. And I was sort of hoping it wasn't just to glower at people and look menacing."

Rick quirked a brow at me. "Why do I get the feeling you're hoping to actually take in this ridiculous money-grab?"

"I mean, carnival games and a show sound kind of fun actually. I know the ringmaster isn't to be trusted, but that doesn't mean the rest of the people here are bad. I've felt his compulsion. For all we know, they'd rather not be here either."

"Just don't go getting it into your head that you're going to liberate people or the animals," he muttered.

"Wouldn't dream of it," I professed, holding my hand to my heart.

Just then, Tyson flagged us down with a stack of papers. I trailed Rick as we closed the distance to the pawn shop proprietor. "Ginny called and said you'd asked to see all of their permits," Tyson said, handing over the stack.

"Trying to catch them in red tape?" I asked.

"In this job you have to be creative."

I couldn't help but give a soft laugh at his words. He was determined to find a way to catch Silvan. It's part of what made Rick a good policeman. He always followed every possible lead until he found the truth. Over the past couple of years, I'd come to appreciate that quality about him, especially as it hadn't been aimed at me in a very long while.

"If you don't mind, I'd like to just wander a bit," I said, gesturing to the row of newly constructed stalls that ran just behind the big top tent.

"I'll keep him company," Tyson offered.

I gave the man a gracious smile and took my leave. As I walked, I couldn't help reflecting on how I'd felt uneasy going into his pawn shop for the first time. I'd been trying to find any clues I could to who might have wanted Vera Chase dead. He'd been so imposing and mercurial then. Now, I just saw him as the businessman he was, shrewd in his dealings with clients. But he had a generous side, too. After all, it had been right here on his land that I'd come out to the town as a witch. For a split second, the sky darkened and the space ahead of me filled with a roaring bonfire. The memory of a lattice of grass emerged from the ground covered in flowers as I showed off my skills.

"You look lost sweetheart," a high-pitched female voice called, pulling me from the memory.

I looked up to find a dark-skinned woman with a short bob standing in front of me. She wore the same athletic pants and mint green top as the woman who'd diverted Silvan's attention. Even in the afternoon light, I could see the sparkling make-up on her cheeks and eyelids that would make her stand out under the bright lights of the big top. She was beautiful.

"Oh, I'm just getting the lay of the land before everything kicks off," I said as I extended my hand, "I'm Darcy."

"Tessa," she replied and gave me a firm shake. "Saw you talking to the cop over there. Hope there's not going to be any trouble."

"Oh, no. He's just here for security. Part of his job and all that," I said.

"You don't look like police to me."

"I'm shadowing him." It wasn't technically a lie since I was here to watch Rick.

"You don't look like you ought to be police either," she added.

"So, are there any rides or stalls that I need to check out while you're here? Like the best ones?" I hoped changing the subject would divert the woman's focus from Rick and his presence.

"Honestly, stay away from the teacup ride. It's been on the fritz for months. They just can't get it fixed right. So, you'd be more likely to get turned with the bumper cars. And The Ferris Wheel is okay, although it gets stuck at the top most of the time. They say it's a quirk of how you can take in the whole rest of the grounds, but really, the motor just sticks."

"Noted."

"I probably shouldn't say anything, but most of the games are rigged. Though if you've got good aim, you can probably win a stuff animal or two off Costello down the end of the row there. Then again, you flash him a flirty smile and he might give you one for free. Just don't tell Silvan. He's a stickler for tracking money coming in and going out."

"The ringmaster said he took over recently after

his cousin passed?" Time to see if the man just had an uncanny family resemblance or if something more nefarious going on.

Tessa's eyes glazed over for a moment. "Yeah .... really sad. Totally unexpected." Her voice was almost robotic. I didn't need to be a witch to see something was off about her response.

After a moment, she blinked, and her gaze refocused on me. "Sorry, what were we talking about?"

"What stalls are worth visiting?"

"The candy apple stall is pretty decent. Lorraine has a special way with all of the candied stuff actually. It's like eating heaven. Well, if it had a flavor, you know?"

"Top of my list then. And what about the show?" I gestured to her outfit. "I've seen a few folks dressed like this. I assume that means you are part of the main event?"

"Everyone comes to the show. We put it on twice a day, and three times on weekends. I don't think you could get away with coming here and not seeing it."

Something told me there was more truth to her words than a casual listener might glean. The main event had to be the biggest ticket value in the whole carnival. I had no doubt Silvan exploited whatever power he had to fill all the seats at every show.

"Well, I'm sure I'll see it at least once, then," I said with a forced smile.

Out of the corner of my eye, I spotted Rick starting to leave Tyson behind. He was heading away from the set up and back towards the center of town. "Sorry, I'd better get going."

Tessa offered me a small wave before she turned her back and disappeared amongst the stalls and machinery beginning to whir to life. I fell into step beside Rick. "Everything in order?"

"Unfortunately," he grumbled. "But that doesn't mean there isn't something off about this whole thing."

"Well, if there is, I know you'll figure it out."

"And something tells me, if I can't, you will."

My cheeks flushed. "I don't know about that."

"Ginny isn't the only one floating the idea of you being something of a detective around town. Vinnie's brought it up, too."

"I'll leave the real police stuff to the professionals. I promise."

As we turned onto the very edge of Main Street, the front flaps to the big top opened and Silvan appeared. His gaze followed us as we moved away from the carnival. Even as the grounds fell out of view, I couldn't shake the sense that the man was still watching us—specifically me. He knew I had magic. Had he known that about Rick, too? Was he drawn to power? It seemed all but certain and I willingly placed myself in his path. *Oh, bloody hell Darcy, what have you gotten yourself into this time?*

4

By five o'clock, Rick had paced the length of his office two dozen times. He kept staring at me like I was an annoyance and part of me wanted to leave the man in peace to brood. But I'd made a promise to Ginny that he wouldn't be left alone while the carnival was in town.

"If you want, I could nip up the street to Ginny's and pick you up something to eat," I offered when he finally flung himself into his chair behind the desk.

"I should be there," he muttered, rubbing at his chin. Either he was ignoring me now or he was too lost in his own musings to have heard my suggestion.

Mercifully, before I needed to repeat myself or ask him what he was going on about, the automatic doors at the front of the station swished open and footsteps echoed on the flooring. I stepped out of Rick's office and gave a sigh of relief when Tania appeared carrying a covered container. My senses picked up on spices that suggested she'd made fresh enchiladas. Maybe we could just keep Rick calm with Tania's cooking.

"I thought you might want a break," Tania suggested. "And Maggie stopped by the B&B asking if you wanted to go the show tonight."

Date night with my girlfriend sounded preferable to babysitting the town's Police Chief. And I had no doubt Tania could keep the man in check.

"You are wonderful," I said and gave my friend a brief embrace.

As if the scent of food were a lure, Rick rolled his chair into the opening of the office. "I could eat. But then, I need to get back to the carnival. I don't trust that Silvan guy farther than I could throw him."

Something told me with his supernatural strength, Rick could throw the ringmaster quite far. Still, I knew he had a reason to be distrustful of the whole enterprise.

"Well, having some dinner in your stomach will help keep you levelheaded," Tania noted before making a shooing gesture in my direction.

"See you around," I called and left the station

behind. I hurried back to the B&B for a quick shower before I went to meet Maggie.

As I left the bathroom, Sam appeared to bar my way down the stairs. In theory, I could just walk through him, but that felt incredibly rude to do to someone I called a friend.

"There is something seriously weird about this carnival," Sam stated solemnly.

"Besides Rick's ingrained distrust of the management?"

"I floated around a bit just to take in the sights. Their costumes are lackluster at best," he sniffed and made a shoulder brushing gesture. As if to say his costumes were far superior. "But it felt like someone was watching *me*."

"People can see you," I reminded him and gestured to the stairs.

He bobbed off to the side to allow me to make my way to the first floor. "Only when I want them to and obviously, I was being sneaky. But something knew I was there."

"Well, it is a magical carnival," I said. "Maybe they've got a medium or a fortune teller or something. Maggie and I are heading there now, so I can keep an eye out."

"If I didn't have to babysit the kitty cop, I wouldn't be going back."

"Be nice. He didn't ask to be a giant cat," I scolded. "And you have the night off. Tania is with Rick for a while."

"Oh, good." I'd never seen such relief wash over his spectral features in the two years since we'd known each other.

"I will keep an eye out for anything strange," I repeated before leaving the B&B behind.

I made it halfway to Maggie's apartment when I spotted her coming in the opposite direction. She smiled at me. "Great minds," she called.

"Tania didn't say where you wanted to meet, so I figured your place was a good spot to start."

"How's Rick holding up?"

"Well, I understand why he loathes Silvan, or whoever the man actually is. He's so ... oily and Sam got bad vibes while he was snooping around. He said he thought someone, or something was watching him even though he was trying very hard not to be seen. And then I talked to one of the performers and when I asked about what happened to the former ringmaster, she got this glazed look on her face."

"Then it's definitely a good idea none of us are going to be alone at this thing." Maggie looped her arm through mine and pulled me close for a kiss. "I'm not going to let anything happen to you."

I wanted to tell her that I wasn't worried about my own safety. But the thought that Silvan knew I had power came rushing back to me the closer we got to the grounds. He'd fundamentally changed Rick without him being able to fight back. Nothing could stop him from doing the same to one of us if he got the idea in his head.

"I know we're on the look-out for danger, but can we try to have some fun tonight too?" Maggie's voice pulled me from my spiral.

"Of course."

Now what attractions had Tessa told me to check out? The Ferris Wheel loomed high above us, the first feature of the carnival to come into view. The sides were lit with bright LED green and blue lights that blinked in an undulating pattern. I heard the whir of motors and laughter as we stepped up to a gate that hadn't been there when Rick and I had left earlier.

"I bought tickets earlier," Maggie explained and held up two small red paper passes that she handed to the gate keeper. He looked at them for a moment before handing them back and placing paper wristbands on our wrists.

"Have fun." His voice was devoid of excitement or any real emotion.

Stepping through the gate was like entering another world entirely. The air felt different as rows of stalls rose up on our right. The rides Tessa had described took up the space to our left. The layout was designed to create a path leading directly to the big top tent. I spotted the stall with stuffed animals and made a mental note to try and win something for Maggie. It was cheesy, but also what couples did at a carnival. And my girlfriend deserved a little quintessential romance.

"I don't think I expected so many people to be here on the opening night," I called above the cacophony of voices and ride music.

"I don't recognize a lot of people," Maggie replied.

I was about to ask how she could possibly know that many locals before remembering that she knew almost everyone in town from her work at the clinic. As I looked around, I realized that I, too, didn't recognize the faces. Except a lone figure caught my attention. I spotted Thomas' head above the fray, his dreads swinging in the wind as he took off at a run towards the entrance to the Ferris Wheel. And if I wasn't mistaken, Sage's shock of blue hair bobbed in and out of view behind the row of stalls to my right.

"How much does the town make from the sales?" I wondered aloud.

"Not a ton. At least not from what Ginny described. But some folks come the whole time the carnival is here. And they don't always want to pay the carnival food prices. So, they come into the town proper to get food and do some shopping. It's definitely a nice boost to the economy."

I stopped people-watching and just let myself enjoy the atmosphere. I was with Maggie and nothing bad was going to happen while we were together. So, I led her down the row of stalls to the one at the end with the stuffed animals. I gestured to the top row and to Maggie, I said, "Pick one."

"Darcy, you don't just get to pick them." The tone of her voice conveyed she thought I'd never been to a carnival before.

I laughed. "I know that. But I need to know what I'm going to win you."

It was her turn to laugh, and she leaned on the

edge of the table in front of us. The man—who I assumed was Costello—watched us intently. Finally, Maggie pointed to a red and blue stuffed dragon. "That one."

Costello looked over his shoulder at her selection then back to me and arched a brow. "Tall order, lass." His Irish accent caught me off guard.

"I'm up for the challenge."

I studied the game in front of me. It was a simple one, knock-the-bottles down with a ball. I had three attempts to do it. Except winning Maggie's desired prize would likely mean I'd need to get it on the first try. Remembering Tessa's words about the games being rigged, I studied the bottles set up across the stall and thought I could make out a thin layer of adhesive running along the bottom row of bottles. As I stood trying to figure out how to compensate for it, I felt my breastbone warm. Tiny shoots of grass were winding their way up behind Costello without me intending it—at least not consciously—to slip their way beneath the bottles.

I glanced towards Maggie, but she hadn't noticed. So, I lined up my shot and flung the ball. It struck the middle row of bottles, sending them toppling along with the one on top. I held my breath as the bottom row wobbled, but stayed standing. I still had two balls remaining. I took a step to my right as the tiny shoots of grass that had managed to slip through the adhesive appeared to shine fluorescent as I moved. They stopped when I had a slightly different angle. Hefting the second ball, I lobbed it overhand. It struck the bottle on the right, wavering before finally tipping backwards. On its way down it bumped the bottle beside it, dislodging whatever Costello had used to secure it on the back table. Only it didn't fall.

"You make this, and I'll give you two dragons," Costello said, clearly believing I was about to walk away empty handed.

Sucking in a breath, I tossed the final ball underhand this time and it bounced off the bottle hard enough to take both it and the ball to the ground. I leaned on the edge of the front table. "So, about those dragons?"

"Lucky shot," he muttered before retrieving two dragons and handing them over. I gave one to Maggie with a curtsy flourish. Armed with our spoils, we resumed our walk along the main thoroughfare towards the big top.

"Don't think I didn't see your little magical assist," Maggie whispered in my ear.

My cheeks burned. "I swear I didn't mean to. It just sort of happened."

"Magic is a powerful thing. And this place is coursing with it. Add that to the fact I'm sure you know these games are rigged, and I'm not surprised it went a little rogue," she replied.

"So, you're not mad?"

Maggie held up her dragon. "I got extra loot out of it."

Relief flooded me as we made our way into the line for the Ferris Wheel. Even if it got stuck, it would still be a nice way to take everything in. The operator stopped the wheel. We climbed into the swaying seat, pulling the security bar down over our laps, and stuffing our prizes in alongside us. The motor whirred and groaned as it brought us up. It gave a sputtering and grinding noise before it stopped entirely leaving our car at the very top of the wheel. I could see everything. I hadn't quite realized just how far the carnival sprawled on Tyson's land. The big top tent took up nearly half the available space. I could make out tall speakers attached to the top of the tent. Just as the wheel began to move, sending us towards the ground again, Silvan's voice blared over the speakers.

"Ladies and gentlemen, please make your way to

the big top for tonight's main attraction. A show of magic and wonder you won't soon forget." Silvan's voice echoed throughout the open air.

"Think we ought to check it out?" Maggie arched a brow at me as the wheel did another loop before coming to a stop at the bottom.

"Absolutely. We want the full carnival experience after all."

We left the rides behind and queued up to get into the tent. Probably fifty people were ahead of us in line. There couldn't be any way they'd all fit inside. And yet when we finally reached the opening and could see the interior, I realized just how big the tent truly was. Audience seats climbed up around the edges in an almost amphitheater style. High above hung a tightrope and trapeze while several rings of light were marking out spaces on the floor.

We found seats midway from the ground on the righthand side. As we settled in, I spotted Rick and Tania a few rows away. Ginny, Tyson, and Vinnie were one behind them. I made eye contact with Tania and mouthed, 'All good?' to which she nodded. Rick looked straight ahead, and I realized he was staring intently at the center ring. Audience members continued to filter through the open tent flaps until every available inch of space was filled with bodies. I craned my neck to see still more people standing in line outside, hoping to catch a glimpse. One would assume there would be another show later in the evening. But it certainly said something about the marketing for the entertainment if literally everyone on the grounds wanted to be in this tent for the very first show of the carnival. Maybe the promise of magic and wonder really did pull people in.

The tent flaps closed, and I could hear a few people give audible groans before they disappeared from view. The lighting in the center of the tent which had illuminated the three rings grew dim, casting the atmosphere into a disorienting gloom. Without realizing it, my focus shifted to the center of the space. Seemingly out of nowhere, Silvan appeared in a red suit with tails and a shiny black top hat. I spotted a lapel mic clipped to his jacket as he turned to survey the crowd. Shadows moved overhead—no doubt performers taking their places for the start of the show.

"My, my, what a wonderful turnout for our opening night. How exhilarating it is to have you all here, poised on the edge of your seat for a show you won't soon forget."

I found myself leaning forward, physically on the

edge of my seat as he spoke. As if his words had the power to force my body to obey. My mind knew this was wrong, and yet I couldn't pull myself away. I managed to cast a sideways look to my left and right. The entire audience was similarly engaged by the ringmaster's words. Everyone except Rick.

5

Focusing on Rick allowed me to slip free of Silvan's enticing opening spiel. I couldn't explain how Rick was immune to the pull of the ringmaster's every word, but he was. I could see the intensity in his glare even from this distance and when the Police Chief turned to look my way, his irises were completely amber. It sent a ripple of anxiety zipping down my spine and settled like a heavy stone in my gut. He might have thought he needed to be here, but it was obviously only serving to upset him.

"Ladies and gentlemen, prepare to be amazed, startled and astounded by the high-flying acts and our death-defying performers," Silvan's voice boomed around the tent, forcing my attention back to the ringmaster.

Still, out of the corner of my eye, I saw Rick clench his hands into tight fists. I couldn't help but fear he was about to lunge from the stands at the ringmaster in center stage. Amongst the crammed seating, I could still feel the earth beneath me, responding to my deeply rooted concern for the man who'd become my friend. Unlike at the stall, I could feel the magic welling up in my core, begging to be let out. This was something I could help Rick with. I was vaguely aware that Silvan continued to speak, rattling off the various acts we'd see during tonight's show, but I focused on feeling the tiny shoots of grass that had been trampled under the weight of the tent and seating. They responded to my presence, longing to be useful and thriving again. I couldn't help but smile at myself as I pictured them gently restraining Rick. I didn't want to harm him. Just give him a reminder that I was here and had his back.

Envisioning the shoots snaking along the ground out of sight and poking up through the seats beside Rick, I poured out a little power. When I opened my eyes, the shoots had lengthened and twisted together into a loose rope-like structure. Slithering snakelike behind the spectators feet, the vine wound its way across to Rick and stopped, as if halted by some other force. He hadn't taken his gaze from Silvan the entire time and my heart skipped a beat at the sudden fear that the ringmaster had somehow ensnared our Chief of Police once more. Swallowing the fear, I mimed looping something loosely around Rick's wrist and watched as the vines curled around the man's wrist.

He blinked and when Rick turned, the amber had all but receded from his gaze. A momentary look of confusion washed over him as he looked at me. He felt the vine around his wrist and gave me a small nod, mouthing what I thought was 'thanks' before turning back to the show. He didn't remove his fingers from the vine.

"Everything okay?" Maggie's voice sounded as if she were speaking through a megaphone.

"I'm fine," I replied, forcing myself to turn my attention back to the show.

Silvan had disappeared from view and all eyes were on the high wire act well above us. I spotted Tessa delicately dancing across the wire, unsupported by any balance aids. It looked like she were floating across solid ground instead of a thin string at least fifty feet in the air.

Trying not to let Rick's strange behavior ruin the evening, I settled into the rhythm of the show. Tessa and her partner—a rail thin woman with bottle blonde hair—floated around one another and my heart stopped when Tessa appeared to flip upside down on the wire. I wasn't the only one to have such a reaction. A ripple of gasps went up from the crowd. Her partner had a grasp on Tessa's wrist somehow and pulled her around. Still, there had to be some sort of magic involved to keep them both from plummeting to the ground.

"It's pretty amazing," Maggie said just loud enough for me to hear this time.

"One might even say magical," I replied, earning a laugh from my girlfriend.

"Look over there," a woman called out from a row below us, pointing off to the far-right ring of light.

I followed the direction she pointed to find a large, uncaged tiger pacing in the spotlight. It didn't move like it was sizing anyone up for dinner. Yet there was still a feral quality to the beast. A stocky man in an over-the-top leotard appeared before the tiger. I half expected him to crack a whip to keep the creature in line, but instead, he bowed to it. The large cat returned the gesture, and they began some sort of practiced routine, mirroring each other's movements in an almost human-like dance.

It took me far too long to put the pieces together. Rick had been turned into a large cat by Silvan—or whatever name he'd gone by then—it made sense he wasn't the first. Granted, I'd only ever seen Rick in an agitated state as a cougar, so I couldn't say whether he'd be as calm and obedient as the tiger down below. But maybe if the circumstances were right, he too retained some of his humanity.

I glanced back in Rick's direction. Where before he'd been just keeping skin contact with the vine, he'd now taken the vine in a vice-like grip. He was visibly shaking. I watched as Ginny reached over and squeezed his shoulder tight. Another touch-point for the man to know that he wasn't alone.

Soon enough, the tiger and his companion vanished. The spotlight swung to the opposite end of the tent to reveal a juggling act who appeared to levitate in mid-air while tossing increasingly dangerous objects overhead. It delighted the crowd around us, but I found myself forgetting about the allure of the magic. My mind couldn't help but try and pick apart how exactly the trick worked.

Clearly, I wasn't Silvan's target audience. I knew too much about how real magic worked to be fooled by the pageantry of it all. Maggie leaned in as the light made a sweep across the tent, momentarily illuminating the rafters before focusing on the next act at ground level.

"Do you see that?" She pointed to something pale overhead.

I turned my gaze upward and squinted. Something almost spectral moved through the space that looked as if it were meant for a trapeze act. But no performers were up there. In fact, the swinging bars looked like they were secured to the tent's scaffolding. And yet, something was definitely up there.

I reached for my phone in my pocket and flipped on the camera. No one had said anything about not using phones, although I would imagine flash photography wasn't exactly the best thing for the performers. Still, I opened my camera app and zoomed in, aiming it at the far end of the trapeze area.

What looked like a giant white cat lounged on a platform in the scaffolding. Except it wasn't a normal housecat and looked more like a lynx. Silvan clearly had a thing for large, wild cats. Still, something was unearthly about the beast. Had this been what Sam sensed watching him before?

No one else seemed to have paid the creature any

mind, all of their attention focused on the main area of the tent where a fire and sword eater stood in the center ring, swallowing swords alight in various shades of flame. People in the audience reacted as the performer appeared to almost choke on a large broadsword.

Even still, I couldn't pull my focus away from the spectral cat high overhead. It caught me looking and its yellow eyes appeared to flash with a strange intelligence. It stretched its front legs out, as if it was preparing to find a better spot to lounge and then took off at a running leap into midair. It seemed to take forever for it to reach the other trapeze platform and for a brief moment, I thought it might simply plummet to the ground.

I blinked and it had vanished from the spot I'd seen it last. I turned in my seat, searching high above in an effort to find it, but it had truly disappeared. I couldn't explain why, but the cat's disappearance sent an uneasy shiver down my spine.

"You don't look like you're enjoying the show," Maggie said, patting my hand to get my attention.

"Honestly, I'm feeling a little off. I'm sorry. I know we wanted to have a nice night," I apologized amid the murmuring oohs and aahs of the entertained crowd around us.

"We can go."

I looked down the row at Rick, Tania, and Ginny. The blonde hadn't let go of her brother's arm and he hadn't lashed out at anyone. So, maybe we were safe to go. Taking a deep breath, I pulled back on my spell and the power that had kept me connected to Rick dissipated. The vine shrunk back from his skin, unwinding strand by strand until it receded back into the ground at his feet. His right arm twitched once, recognizing the absence of the vine, but it wasn't enough to pull Rick's focus my way.

"I think I just need some air," I suggested. So, Maggie and I picked our way through the stands to the entrance of the tent.

I half-expected the muscled carnival staff, possibly a strong man to be posted outside ready to keep patrons inside just as much ensuring no one else snuck in. Yet, no one was waiting. I pushed my way through the thick canvas flap and sucked in a gulp of air.

The sky had gone dark since we'd stepped inside the tent, and I could see stars winking in the distance. Lights on the rides sparkled brighter in the dimness. People still queued up for rides and game booths, hoping to win something. Maggie slid her hand into mine and led me back down the main thoroughfare between the stalls offering games and chances to win prizes.

"Feeling any better?" She asked softly as our pace slowed to a meander.

"Yeah. Some weird things were going on in there. Like, I'm pretty sure that tiger had to be a shifter. Even a kept animal, trained to do a routine, wouldn't behave that human. And I'm pretty sure the tight rope performers were using some sort of magic to stay up there."

"Well, we knew the carnival was full of magic, right?"

"I know. I guess I was just expecting them to hide it more. Pretty silly when that's the whole bloody draw of the show," I muttered.

"I will admit, I think there was something off about the ringmaster. I could feel a sort of enticing pull when he was speaking," Maggie added.

"It's like he speaks, and whoever is listening will believe whatever he says," I noted. "Perfect power for someone in the entertainment business."

I spotted a bench in between a couple of unattended booths and led Maggie to sit down. We could just enjoy some people-watching until the main show ended. I didn't feel comfortable leaving the carnival while Rick was still on the grounds.

Not with the way he'd reacted to Silvan's opening words.

"Part of me had thought that maybe we were overreacting before, about not wanting Rick to be alone while the carnival was here," I began. Maggie turned to look me in the eyes. "But the way he reacted, I worried he was going to jump out of the stands. I've never seen him like that."

"It has to be triggering for him. But he has a solid support system to keep him steady. And don't think I missed what you did for him."

I let out a soft laugh. "Can't get anything by you today, can I?"

She leaned in and planted a kiss on my lips. "Nope."

"Did you find anything creepy?" Sam's voice made me jump and I found him bobbing in mid-air behind the bench.

"Bloody hell, mate. Don't scare a girl like that."

He gave me a playful eye roll before his expression went serious. "I can feel it still, watching."

"I saw something a bit strange in the tent. It looked like a ghostly cat, and it definitely knew I was watching it," I confirmed. "But it didn't really interact with anyone else. In fact, after it noticed me watching, it disappeared entirely."

Sam gave a full-body shiver that made his translucent form ripple. "I hate cats. Never liked them, even when I was alive."

"Yeah, well this one was definitely spooky," I agreed.

Just then, voices drifted down the thoroughfare and I could see a steady stream of people moving away from the big top. Had the show ended already? I checked my phone; it was after nine o'clock. People streamed by and I scanned the crowd for familiar faces. I got a small wave from Thomas as he passed, but he wasn't who I was looking for.

The throng thinned faster than I would have thought and still I hadn't spotted Ginny, Tania, Vinnie, or Rick. My pulse thrummed uncomfortably in my throat as I searched every face. Finally, I spotted my landlady and Vinnie approaching us. They couldn't hide the panic in their expressions.

"Where's Rick?" The words flew out of my mouth.

"We ... we don't know," Vinnie answered.

"What—what do you mean you don't know? He was sitting with you and Ginny when we left," Maggie interjected.

I was on my feet. "What happened?"

"The final act came out, but there appeared to be some confusion," Tania explained. "The ringmaster was supposed to come out again at some point, and he didn't. The other performers did their best to wrap things up, but it was about that time I realized Rick wasn't sitting next to me anymore."

"Maybe he and Ginny left?" The tinge of hope in my voice felt fake even to me.

"He's not anywhere I can find," Ginny's voice called from the other direction as she approached.

"This isn't that big a place. He couldn't have gone far," I said.

"Maybe not on two legs," Ginny pointed out.

I flashed back to the pure amber of his irises at the start of the show. The way he'd barely constrained himself. Rick was full of distrust and rage at the man who had forever changed his life.

"You said the ringmaster wasn't there at the end. We need to find where his office is or wherever he stays. Maybe Rick's there?" I took off before I'd finished speaking with the others trailing me.

We made it back to the stall where I'd won the dragons for Maggie and I. Costello leaned against the front edge of the stall. "Back for another shot, lass?"

"We're looking for someone. We think they might be with Silvan. Where would we find him?"

"Finishing up in the big top."

"No, we just came from the show. He wasn't present at the end of the performance," Vinnie stepped up, putting on his stern cop voice. "Where else might he be?"

Costello looked nervous for a beat before gesturing behind the tent. "He's got a caravan back there. Uses it as his office."

I took off at a run, only to be outpaced by Ginny. Our group rounded the far end of the tent, and I could see a camper sitting hooked up to a generator just behind the tent. I picked up on the smell of something visceral as we approached. I reached for Maggie's hand as we slowed to a walk and inched around the edge of the camper. Silvan was sprawled on the ground, a bloody mess. Someone scrambled in the dirt behind the camper, and we pivoted as one to find Rick curled up against the metal paneling, naked with his hands covered in blood.

6

I tore my eyes away from the dead man, trying hard not to commit the injuries to memory. Instead, I focused all of my attention on Rick. He looked disoriented and almost feral. There was a healthy glint of amber still ringing his irises as Ginny approached him.

"Rick, can you hear me?" Her voice was low, non-threatening.

He blinked rapidly, as if struggling to process her words. A moment or two later, he nodded slowly. Still, he didn't speak.

"We need to cover him up," Maggie said.

"No, we can't disturb a crime scene," Vinnie retorted.

"I was talking about Rick," she replied sharply.

She tugged off her jacket and offered it to Ginny who artfully positioned it over her brother's body.

"What do we do?" I asked, looking at Vinnie.

He let out a slow breath. "Well, normally, I'd say call in the authorities, but, uh ... well, we're already here."

Ginny stood and faced the rest of us. "I know how this all looks, but even at his angriest, Rick wouldn't do this."

I didn't want to argue with her, but based on the behavior I'd witnessed, and the fact Rick had been able to slip free of their attention told a different story. I swallowed the doubt rising in my throat.

"I know none of us want to believe he could have done this. But Ginny, did you see how he looked in there when Silvan was giving his opening spiel? Rick looked positively scary."

"He was fine until you left," she snapped. "Your little vine spell kept him anchored. And then you just got up and walked out abandoning him."

"He had you. From what I could see, you were doing just as much to ground him. But I wasn't the one who lost track of him."

"Enough!" Tania's voice cut through the arguing. "We will accomplish nothing by accusing each other. That is not what Rick needs from us right now." She turned to Vinnie. "We will stay here until you come back."

"And where is he going?" Ginny snapped.

"I need to find out who is in charge of the carnival in Silvan's absence. Also, I need to notify them that he's dead," Vinnie answered somberly. He made a vague gesture to the space around us. "And I'm going to the car to get some tape to cordon off the area. Do not touch anything."

I took a step or two away from the dead man and Rick still hunched against the back of the camper. He'd remained mute this entire time. I would have expected him to jump in to defend himself. Instead, he looked confused. The supernatural tinge to his eyes had receded some with his humanity reasserting itself, but it wouldn't surprise me if he were in shock.

"We're not going to lie for him," Maggie blurted unprompted. Her words drawing our collective attention.

"We don't know what happened. So, there's nothing to lie about," Ginny retorted.

"I think what Maggie meant is that we need to be open to seeing where this goes. Even if it means we aren't going to like the answers," I explained.

"I'm telling you; he didn't do it."

"Ginny, please look at this situation objectively," I pressed. "We all know he had motive. And frankly, having met Silvan, I don't blame Rick for hating the man. He had the opportunity. I mean, clearly everyone else was distracted and wouldn't notice him missing for a while."

"And he had the means, being in the right frame of mind," Maggie added.

"I think ... I think I did it," Rick mumbled, holding up his hands.

"Shh ... brother you're in shock," Ginny said in a mothering fashion. "We don't know anything yet."

Just then, Vinnie returned with the yellow crime scene tape. He secured one end to the edge of the camper and unwound it, giving the body a wide berth as he came around the far end of the camper.

"You should see if you can find Tessa. It seemed like she knew a lot about what was going on in the carnival," I suggested to Vinnie, when he'd pocketed the roll of tape.

"Thanks. Just ... stay here. I know it's going to sound ridiculous, but I am going to need all of your statements about the evening."

I watched Vinnie disappear again, and I noted the slight slump in his shoulders. He was not expecting to have to lead an investigation all on his own. And until we figured out what had happened and how Rick fit into the narrative, Vinnie had no choice but to run point. Still, I knew he was fully capable of taking the reins.

While Ginny continued to fuss over Rick, I forced myself to take stock of the dead body in the cordoned off area. The grass around Silvan was definitely trampled, and I thought I could make out something like shoe impressions in the dirt. But that could have been easily left from when they were setting up. Nothing suggested the prints were made as part of an attack.

I didn't know a whole lot about crime scene analysis—just what I'd picked up from the odd detective show—but it didn't appear Silvan had been moved to this spot after he'd died. So, this had to be the place where he'd been killed. It was relatively secluded and if we hadn't been looking for Rick, there was no telling how long it would have taken for someone to discover the ringmaster behind the trailer. Part of me wanted to use my magic to see if I could catch a glimpse back into what had happened, but I couldn't force myself to take that step. The man's body was awash in blood and mangled flesh. I didn't want or need to see that scene.

"Something with pretty big claws made those wounds," Maggie assessed from beside me.

"Like a cougar perhaps?" I rasped.

"Maybe. Or it could have been someone with some sort of handheld weapon, like Wolverine."

I shook my head. "No, I think you're right and it was claws that dug in." My stomach lurched.

"I know it looks bad right now, but there has to be an explanation."

"And sometimes the right answer is the simplest." It was entirely possible our Chief of Police had let his animal instincts get the better of him and finally gotten revenge on the man who'd changed his life forever.

"I don't see any defensive wounds," I said after a moment. I had shifted my gaze down to Silvan's hands and forearms. Surely, he'd have put up a fight if someone he hadn't seen in years had attacked him with the intention of doing harm.

"There's a lot of blood. It's probably obscuring them," Maggie murmured.

Heavy footsteps put an end to our assessment, and we turned to find Vinnie leading Tessa to us. "I'm so sorry to have to report that Silvan's dead."

Upon seeing the body, Tessa let out a gasp and

covered her face, turning away immediately. "This can't be happening," she moaned.

"I know this could be difficult, but I am going to need you to shut down the carnival until we can sort out what happened. And I'll need to speak with all of your staff."

"You think one of us, did it?" she asked through a sob.

"I just need to establish where everyone was at the time he died."

"You think it's foul play ... That he was murdered?"

"Unfortunately, and until I can prove otherwise, yes. I think he died under suspicious circumstances."

Tessa wiped at her eyes and angled her body, so she wasn't looking at Silvan's prone form. Except it gave her a perfect vantage point to see Rick still huddled and bloody by the trailer—inside the crime scene tape's perimeter.

"How can you accuse one of us of murder when you've got someone with bloody hands sitting right there?" she demanded.

Vinnie moved to block Rick from her sight line. "I promise you; we will be looking at everything. For now, I need you to close things down. But everyone that is still here, even visitors, they need to stay put."

"I knew coming here was a mistake," Tessa muttered as she disappeared.

Vinnie's exhale of breath was audible as he looked back over to Rick and Ginny. "Chief, I'm really sorry about this. But I'm going to need to have you taken into the station for processing."

Rick nodded, more with it this time. "I understand." He blinked slowly. "You should get crime techs out here. They shouldn't process me at the station though. Too much of a chance I could transfer evidence and contaminate the chain of custody."

Vinnie rubbed at the nape of his neck. "Right. Uh, you're right."

I pulled Vinnie aside as he fished his phone out of his pocket. "Is there anyone else we should call? An outside department? I mean, I'm rooting for Rick not to have done this. But anyone with an ounce of common sense is going to see this as a conflict of interest a mile off."

Vinnie shook his head. "No way I'm handing this off to anyone else. They can question my judgment all they want. I'm not going to go easy on Rick just because he's my boss and my friend. He trained me better than that."

"Yeah, but I mean, we all know Rick had a reason

to go after the ringmaster. He looks pretty guilty, and I worry any one of us would try to find a way to make it not the case if we could."

"You have my word, Darcy. I'm not going to let my emotions get in the way of investigating this one. And honestly, I could use your help." He made a vague gesture towards the scene. "... figuring out what you might be able to glean. You know?"

"The thought crossed my mind. But I don't know if I'm ready to see that."

"Oh, right. I shouldn't ask that of you. I'm sorry. I just ... I know it's going to be a long night, and I need help. And maybe your magic might be an ... an easy way to see what we're dealing with."

I could put aside my own unease about watching a man get murdered if it helped my friends. It wouldn't be the first time I'd witnessed a crime through the eyes of the living foliage around a body.

"Okay, okay I'll do it. For Rick. But ... I think I need a little space to clear my head first."

"It's not going anywhere."

"Maybe we could at least get Rick something to wear for when the crime scene team gets here? They don't need to see him naked."

"A little nudity never killed anyone," Rick called

from behind me. "I'm not risking contaminating anything."

I pivoted to look at the man. He'd shifted himself into more of a seated position with his legs outstretched in front of him. He still held his hands above Maggie's jacket, careful not to touch anything. "Rick, do you remember anything about what happened?"

"You don't have to answer that," Ginny jumped in.

"You're not a lawyer, Gin. And Darcy isn't police," Rick replied, giving his sister a dismissive look.

"Ginny, I know we all feel like we let him down. I swear I'm just trying to help," I said with a placating hand gesture.

"I know you're not trying to interrogate him," Ginny admitted in a defeated tone. "I just thought we were going to be okay. I hoped we could get through the carnival being here after I screwed up and let them in."

"Silvan was clearly very good at concealing things. If Rick was right and he really was the same man who'd turned him all those years ago, he could have just as easily manipulated you into believing whatever he said," I pointed out.

"Darcy and I were saying earlier it felt like the

ringmaster had some sort of pull over the audience in there," Maggie agreed.

Tania had remained quiet and purely an observer to this point. A far-off look was in her eyes, as if she were lost somewhere in her thoughts. I stepped closer to my landlady and gave her a gentle nudge with my shoulder. "Everything alright?"

"I could sense Rick's fear and his anger while we were in the big top. Both reasonable emotions given the circumstances. But I never felt a surge of anything that would have signaled he'd snapped in any way."

"I don't remember snapping either," Rick offered. "I remember Darcy's little vine. It was like a lifeline, keeping me grounded."

"And then I needed to get out of there ... needed air. So, I let the magic go and took that away from you. I'm sorry."

"Don't apologize. You all shouldn't have had to babysit me," he muttered.

Just then, I heard tires crunching over the grass and saw the crime scene tech van approaching. Almost simultaneously, Tessa's voice came over the loudspeaker.

"Ladies and gentlemen, I am very sorry to report there has been an incident on the grounds. The police are investigating and have asked that you stay on the premises until you have spoken with them."

She sounded calm, even-tempered. Not at all like the woman who'd gone off a few minutes earlier, sobbing and accusing Rick of murder. I tried not to dwell on the strange shift in her behavior as the techs marched over with Vinnie trailing them.

"Start with processing the chief," Vinnie explained.

The techs shared a surprised look before ducking carefully under the tape and settling beside Rick. He kept his hands where they could see them and didn't flinch as they started scraping the blood from his hands. I watched from a safe distance, trying to catch any glimpse that might suggest he'd been injured in a struggle or that the claws I knew he sported in his shifted form had dug into another man's flesh and muscle.

Before long, the techs obscured my view and Vinnie pulled Ginny from Rick's side. He spoke with her quietly a short distance away, his notepad in hand. He was getting to work. Not like he had any other choice in the matter.

"You're going to help Vinnie sort this whole mess out," Maggie said. There wasn't a hint of questioning in her tone.

"It's Rick. Despite all the discomfort we had at the start of my coming here, he's a good man. He is good at what he does, and this time he deserves to have us figure out what happened. No matter what the outcome is."

"Tell me how I can help."

"Vinnie wants me to see what I can glean from the surrounding area. But I'm scared of what I'll find. I don't want to do it alone. Maybe two pairs of eyes are better than one?"

"You think we can figure out a way for me to tag along on your little plant-fueled vision quest."

Knowing I was going to have Maggie with me bolstered my resolve. This night had not gone at all how any of us had expected, but there was no chance we were going to let Rick go down for something he didn't do. Now I just had to pray there was some other explanation for why the man with a strong motive had wound up covered in a dead man's blood.

7

I knew sleep would help prepare me to use my magic and assess the scene for Vinnie. And yet, I couldn't bring myself to close my eyes. I lay in bed beside Maggie at her apartment as the clock ticked past one in the morning. Every time I closed my eyes, I saw Silvan's prone form, bloody and cold lying in the grass. And Rick huddled nearby, looking feral. I didn't want to believe that he had done this, but part of me still couldn't shake the idea. After all, Rick didn't even believe he wasn't responsible. Realizing sleep was fruitless, I quietly crept out of bed and went through the open floor plan to Maggie's kitchen and busied myself with brewing a pot of coffee. If I wasn't going to sleep, I might as well give myself some extra stimulation.

"Shouldn't you be getting your beauty sleep?" Sam's voice only made me jump a little.

"Would if I could, mate."

"Can't get that creep's face out of your head?"

"More like the horrible wounds in his torso. And seeing Rick like that ... honestly, it was scary."

"Yeah, but you knew what he turned into. You'd seen him transform before."

"Yeah, but that was different. I mean, for one thing he wasn't really in control of his body at the All Hallows Eve Extravaganza. Someone else was literally in the driver seat. This time ... it was all him, Sam."

"Yeah, it was." I picked up on the slight hint of suggestion in his tone and glared at him. He offered a dismissive shrug in return. "You can't just leave that hanging out there and expect me to ignore it."

"You're just making it worse. Please stop," I begged as the coffee pot began to percolate behind me. "Besides, I have no idea how I'm meant to bring Maggie along on this spell Vinnie's asked me to do at the crime scene."

"Wish I had an answer. Poor guy's been out there all night interviewing people."

"None of this is fair to put on just him. I get

wanting to keep things close, at least until we know what happened with Rick. But Vinnie is only one person. He can't do it all on his own."

"Well, he's basically deputized you and Maggie. Even if he didn't use those exact words."

"Is it wrong of me to think ... I'm not too broken up if Rick did really do it? I mean, if Silvan is the man Rick thought he was, that had to open up a lot of old wounds. Lesser men have snapped over much smaller life altering encounters."

"If you ask me, you're not wrong for thinking the prick deserved it."

That seemed an odd choice of words for Sam to use. It wasn't like he had any interactions with Silvan. "You didn't have any past experiences with the ringmaster, did you?"

"No. But while I was snooping around, before whatever that thing was that could sense me spooked me, I heard him talking to some of his performers."

"Talking about what?"

"Honestly, I wasn't that interested. It was about a trapeze or something not working right. He sounded mad about it. But the way he talked to them was really controlling. He might put on a nice guy face for the crowd, but it sounded to me like everyone working for him could have a reason to off the guy."

I filed that bit of information away for later. My mind wasn't sharp enough right now to do much else with it. "That's all well and good, but it still doesn't assist me in helping Vinnie or Rick."

"I thought I heard voices out here," Maggie called sleepily, appearing in the doorway from the bedroom. She made a beeline for the coffee pot as it finished brewing. "Can't sleep?" She held out a mug to me.

I took the mug and held it close to my face, inhaling the bitter aroma of the coffee. "I tried, really I did. I just can't get the dead man out of my head. Also, I have no idea how I'm going to bring you along when I try to see what the plants saw ... I don't want to let anyone down. I suppose I'm just feeling a bit overwhelmed."

Maggie pulled me into a one-armed hug while she held her own mug. "Well, there's no pressure from me. I want to be there to support you and help manage things, but if it is going to be too problematic, then I am fine stepping out."

"No, I want you there. I do. I just ... don't understand how it would even work. I've never tried to share this part of my magic with anyone before." The more I thought about it, the more I realized up until this point, my magic had been a solitary endeavor. Yes, I'd had Maggie and Tania for support, but the feats I'd achieved were only on my own.

"I might have an idea or two. It's sort of a combination of some herbal enhancements and deep breathing. Nothing invasive, but it should get us more in sync with each other."

"That sounds lovely," I replied.

"As for getting you some actual sleep, I have something for that, too."

I expected her to whisk away the coffee and give me some of her chamomile tea. Except Maggie went rummaging in a different cupboard by the sink and came away with a small jar of bright yellow powder. She made a grabbing gesture for my mug, and I handed it over. I watched her quizzically as she spooned three large portions into my coffee, gave it a solid stir, and the powder vanished.

"I'm surprised you're not pouring chamomile tea down my throat," I noted.

"Well, there is a time and place for the gentle method. This should knock you on your butt in a matter of an hour. And it should help with any bad dreams, too."

After the night we'd all had, that sounded brilliant. I downed the coffee, only recoiling slightly at the last dregs of powder that hadn't completely dissolved. Maggie took the mug from my hands and guided me back to the bedroom. I was already feeling sluggish and sleepy by the time we made it to bed again. I curled up beneath the blanket and felt Maggie settle in beside me, draping an arm across my torso.

I SHOULDN'T HAVE DOUBTED MAGGIE. WHEN IT CAME to healing potions and tinctures, she was a miracle worker. I woke five hours later feeling as if I'd gotten a full night's rest and no hint of last night's trauma and carnage had haunted my dreams. For a split second, I considered asking Maggie for some more to take again. Though given that she'd not brought it out during the half dozen mysteries we'd been mixed up in over the last year, I suspected this was a one and done spell.

"You look better," she noted when I emerged from the bathroom. A plate of eggs and toast sat on the table in the kitchen area. She made a small gesture towards the plate.

"You weren't kidding that stuff knocked me right out."

"Good."

"Once we finish up here, I think we ought to head back to the carnival grounds and see if we can get a sense of what happened. I'm sure Vinnie could use a break."

"I've been thinking. Maybe it would be easier for you not to try bringing me along," Maggie suggested, brushing a loose strand of hair behind her ear.

"No, I want you there. We don't know exactly what we're going to see, but I'd rather it be something we share. That way we could work through it together. Last night, I was just in shock by what happened. That's all."

She gave a silent nod before settling in with a plate of her own. By the time we'd finished our meal and set the dishes to soak in the sink, my phone read almost eight o'clock. I stowed my phone in my pocket, and we retraced our route down Main Street to the edge of Tyson's property.

The grounds were surprisingly busy given the early hour and the tragedy that had struck last night. Carnival performers and other staff milled about the place, tending to the rides and restocking stalls with prizes. Though I doubted Vinnie had given them the okay to continue having visitors until Silvan's death was solved. Thankfully, none of them paid much attention to us as we made our way past the big top and behind Silvan's trailer. The police tape still waved in the wind, but stayed secure where Vinnie had left it. I could feel bile threatening to rise up my throat. For a split second, Silvan's body superimposed itself over the space, his unseeing gaze staring up at me. I blinked and the body vanished. I looked around the area in an effort to assess where the killer might have come from and what way they must have been facing when the attack happened.

"Tell me how I can help." Maggie's voice anchored me.

"I'm just trying to figure out the best place to pull the plant's memories from. I mean literally each blade of grass has its own story to tell. But where do I start?"

"Well, we know Silvan was lying this way when we came upon him. And Rick was over there," Maggie gestured to the space directly in front of us. "And from what I could see of the wounds, the attack was front on. So, if we want a chance to see the killer's face, I think trying to see as much from Silvan's vantage point as possible is our best option."

Her logic made sense, and I made my way around the perimeter of the crime scene, careful not to tread on anything that could be important later. I didn't see any boot impressions in the grass, so maybe whoever had taken down the ringmaster had come barefoot. It would certainly be plausible, especially if that someone could change form.

Time to get this over with.

I reached for Maggie's hand and held it tight while bending down and brushing the fingertips of my free hand along the blades of grass in front of me.

"Breathe with me now. If we're in sync, I think it should be easier for your magic to recognize mine and include me in what you're trying to do," Maggie instructed.

She pulled my hand to her chest, and I felt her heart thumping steadily against her breastbone. She reached out with her other hand and pressed it to mine. In a matter of minutes our breathing and heartbeats were in unison.

'I know you can hear me. I need to see what happened here. Show me the man who died. Show me how it happened. And let Maggie see, too.'

My vision went green at the edges as I began to see through the plants' memory. The world grew dark around us, and it was as though someone had put a recording on rewind at double speed. I could see Vinnie and the crime scene investigators prodding around Silvan's body and escorting Rick from the scene. Ginny and Tania went with the chief. Time continued to reverse until Maggie and I appeared on the scene, discovering the body.

"Whoa, this is ... unreal," Maggie whispered.

That was all the confirmation I needed to know the magic was working the way it was supposed to. Finally, the spectral images of our search party vanished. Time continued to rewind, but Rick simply loomed over Silvan's body. I could see his hands pressed to the man's chest where the wounds had been inflicted.

'Go back farther.'

The blades of grass beneath my fingers quivered, as if the request was physically painful to obey. And yet, time rewound more until Silvan vanished from sight. Finally, the timelapse ceased and started to play forward at normal speed. Silvan appeared around the edge of the trailer with a confused expression on his face. He said something, but I couldn't make it out. He was facing where we stood, and his confusion soon turned into something akin to irritation. He made a waving off gesture and turned to leave when something like an intense soundwave rippled through the air.

Silvan spun to look at the origin of the sound and his eyes went wide. In a flash he was lying on the ground, his shirt ripped open, and bloody wounds weeping already. He struggled against his assailant, who moved far too fast to be seen. But something was off about the attacker. It didn't look like the tawny coloring of a cougar. Well, not entirely anyway. All I could discern was the killer moved catlike and agile on its feet. And it took off like a shot when Silvan stopped moving.

I scanned our surroundings, waiting for Rick to emerge as I'd seen him do in reverse. After what felt like ages, he appeared naked and running. But not from the direction I'd seen the creature disappear. It was as if he were coming from the opposite direction. He, too, looked confused by his surroundings. He dropped to his knees at the sight of the dead man, pressing his hands to the man's chest.

I pulled my hand free of the greenery beneath me and the images faded away. I blinked a time or two to clear the green tinge from my vision and sunk back on my heels. Maggie let out a breath beside me and I gave her hand a squeeze.

"I don't think Rick did it," Maggie blurted.

"We can't be sure though," I replied and pulled myself to my feet. "Yeah, it looked like he was trying to stop the bleeding. But that doesn't mean he didn't lose it in his shifted form and then was remorseful after the fact. Or maybe he didn't intend to attack him, but it just happened?"

"The way he moved suggested he was surprised by what he'd come across," Maggie pressed. "We should talk to Rick now that he's had a chance to get his head straight. We need to know what he remembers."

"Did you feel that soundwave right before Silvan was attacked?" I looked at the empty space behind us, trying to gauge where the creature could have been lying in wait. Nothing stood out.

"That was so strange," Maggie answered. "It was like it had actual form. And whatever it was definitely caught Silvan's attention."

I made a mental note to revisit the carnival and ask around about what other secrets this place might be keeping just out of sight.

"I think you're right, though. Rick should be our next stop."

As we left the scene behind, a feeling of being watched nagged at me. I turned back and thought I caught the small curtain along the front window of

Silvan's trailer flutter, as if someone was watching us. I stopped, waiting for more movement but nothing did. I tried to play it off as a trick of the light. Yet as we left the carnival behind, I couldn't shake the sense of foreboding wrapping around me like an unwanted, weighted blanket.

8

Returning to Main Street it felt eerie as Maggie and I walked side by side towards the police station. In contrast with the hustle and bustle of the carnival, the rest of town was too quiet. Far more people should have been out and about at this hour, even if they were just heading for a weekend breakfast at Ginny's. Maybe the murder had spooked everyone and convinced them to stay home. I had little doubt that Rick being questioned would spread through town like wildfire.

The station came into view, and I spotted Ginny standing outside, a to-go cup in her hand and a paper bag tucked under one arm. Her cheeks were pale, and she didn't react when Maggie and I approached.

"Did you get any sleep last night?" I asked quietly, attempting not to startle her.

"I tried, but I didn't manage more than a few minutes," she admitted. "I wanted to stay with Rick, but he basically kicked me out." She let out a bitter laugh. "Even from the holding cell, he's still running the place."

"We went by the scene this morning. We've got some questions we want to ask him. I'm sure he'd appreciate the coffee and food," I said, gesturing to the cup and bag.

"Uh, yeah ... I just haven't been able to bring myself to go in yet."

I held out a hand to take the bag from her. "So, don't go in alone."

She handed it over and gave me a sad smile. "I know I kind of took your head off last night. I shouldn't have."

"We were all under a lot of stress. I'd be lying if I didn't blame myself a little, too."

With that, we walked three abreast through the automatic doors into the station. It was silent, not even the whir of the air conditioning filled the space. Rick sat behind bars in the station's single holding cell. At least someone had gotten him a pair of sweatpants and a t-shirt with the Brookhaven Police

Department crest on it. He sat at the back of the cell with his head resting against the cinderblock wall that abutted the evidence room.

"We thought you might be hungry," I called and held up the bag that smelled suspiciously like a sausage and egg breakfast sandwich.

He opened his eyes and looked at me. The scruff on his cheeks and chin made him look almost rugged as he sat up. "I shouldn't accept it but, hell, I'm starving."

I passed the bag through the bars and Ginny handed him the coffee. "You look better."

"You look worse," he commented, and she ducked her head.

"Has Vinnie been by to process you?"

"Not yet. The crime scene boys finished up hours ago and let me change before I locked myself in here. But I suspect he'll be by soon to take my statement."

"Before he does, we were hoping we could ask you a couple of questions," I said and leaned on the cold metal bars separating us. "Maggie and I went back to the crime scene and things don't exactly add up from what we saw."

He blinked at me, confusion clouding his brown irises. "What you saw?"

"Vinnie asked me to take a look around with my magic. So, that's what I did. Maggie came along as support and honestly, two sets of eyes are better than one. Silvan wasn't alone. That much is clear. But we couldn't see who he was talking to. And then, there was a strange sound wave. Whoever killed him tackled him to the ground before running off."

"But then you showed up. It looked like you were trying to help him," Maggie added. "The blood on your hands was from trying to stop the bleeding."

Rick looked at his hands, flexing his fingers and rubbing them together as if he could still feel the slickness of the man's blood on his skin. "I've been trying to piece it all together, but things are still hazy."

"Why not start with what you do remember?" I suggested and turned to Ginny. "Is there anything you can do to make sure what he's saying is the truth?"

She gave another bitter laugh. "I'm pretty sure Rick is the one person it doesn't work on."

"I've just never had a reason to lie to you, Gin," Rick answered. "But I think my sister just being here will help."

"So, go back to when things are clear. What do you remember most?"

"I remember going to the carnival and sitting with Tania and Ginny at the show. I honestly thought about skipping it, but I realized that would give that man more power over me. And I wasn't going to let that happen. So, I forced myself to go."

"Do you remember me grounding you?" I pressed.

He rubbed at his wrist. "I do. It helped. I had this strange feeling as Silvan was speaking, he was trying to lull me into some sort of spell. But it wasn't me that was reacting. The creature inside was what was responding to him. I'd never had that happen before. At least not that I could remember."

"After I left and the plant lifeline faded, what do you remember?"

Rick rubbed at the nape of his neck deep in thought. "I had this sense that I needed to get some air. Everyone else around me was so taken, and lost in the show, it was easy to slip out."

Part of me wondered if there had been some residual connection between us and my own emotions had influenced his desire to leave. I kept quiet and let him continue speaking.

"Once I was out in the air, I thought I heard Silvan talking again. And it was like the creature inside of me responded again. I took off, trying to follow him, like I was drawn to him. And I think at some point, I shifted. Because things went, uh ... primal. I could see and smell everything around me, but somehow, I knew there wasn't much higher order thinking. It was just instinct."

"Where did you make the change?" I pressed. "You had no clothes on when we found you, so I'm assuming you took them off."

"I don't remember. I think there weren't many people around though."

"What direction did you go when you left the tent? Was it towards the rides or the stalls?" Maggie jumped in.

"I think it was towards the rides. But honestly, like I said, it's a blur."

"If you were going towards the rides, that's the opposite direction of where Silvan was found. Do you remember what drew you there?"

"Once I am in my shifted form, the cat just takes over and, a lot of the time, I'm not really present. But I think there was something ... a sound or a smell ... it drew me there. I remember seeing something run by me. It was definitely on four legs and smelled feline."

"What made you shift back to human form?" Ginny's voice shook as she asked the question.

"Whatever had drawn me in disappeared and I

was compelled to shift back. I think that's when I found him lying next to the camper bleeding."

"And you've never felt that sort of pull to change before?" I pressed my hands against the cell's bars.

"Not that I can recall. Not even when I first transformed years ago."

"It had to be the proximity to Silvan and the rest of the carnival," Maggie suggested.

"You said you sensed something feline," I said, redirecting the conversation. "We saw a tiger in the show. And it had left the tent by the time Maggie and I went for air. The beast moved like it was more human than animal during the show."

"It's possible. I didn't really get a good look or sense of it. But it was definitely cat-like."

There was also the spectral cat I'd seen in the rafters by the trapeze. It had given me an unsettling sense of being watched. I wasn't sure it could actually interact with anything physical though. But supernatural ghosts could possess living beings. We'd seen that with Ginny's spell at Halloween.

Before I could broach the subject with Rick or the others, the doors behind us opened and a bedraggled Vinnie walked in. He clearly hadn't slept either and the wrinkles in his uniform suggested he hadn't even gone home for a change of clothes.

"You find anything?" he asked, looking directly at me.

"Just that something with four legs and nasty claws likely killed Silvan. And it gave off some sort of really intense sound before it attacked."

"Sound?"

"I don't know exactly. I was looking at it through the grass' sense memory. It doesn't actually hear words. But the killer got Silvan's attention. And he was talking to whoever or whatever it was before he died."

"I'm not the best at lip reading, but it looked as if he said something like, 'I'm done arguing,'" Maggie interjected.

And this was why I was grateful Maggie had been along on this one with me. Not only could we share the burden of seeing Silvan's murder, but she'd picked up on details I'd missed. I looked at Rick. "If that's right, would you have understood what he said to you in your shifted form?"

Rick shook his head. "No."

"Then Rick couldn't have done it," I declared, earning me an arched brow from Vinnie.

"I don't want it to be true either," he began.

"Listen. Rick will tell you when you interview him, but he shifted somewhere else on the other side of the carnival. Silvan was already dead by the time he showed up."

Vinnie looked at Rick with a hopeful expression. "That true, chief?"

"Something compelled me to shift and then change back. I sensed something else feline running away from the scene. I think Darcy is right and I had his blood on my hands from when I tried to stop the bleeding."

"We're still waiting for the lab to process the evidence, but if it wasn't you, then it would make my investigation so much easier," Vinnie proclaimed.

"Yeah, but if Rick didn't do it, then who did?" Ginny pressed.

"Well, there is that tiger," Maggie reminded her. "I mean I highly doubt Rick was the first person to shift forms at this carnival, especially if they're the ones who changed Rick in the first place."

"And there's the weird spectral cat Sam and I saw," I added.

"Spectral cat?" The question came from inside the holding cell. "What are you talking about?"

"Yeah, I didn't see anything," Ginny agreed.

"I don't know. It looked like a lynx or something, but it was definitely a ghost. I could see through it, like I can with Sam. And it looked like it was just lurking up in the rafters. But it spotted me and took off. And when Sam was looking around yesterday, he said he felt something watching him even though he was purposely making sure no one would notice him."

"I've never seen any ghostly cats running around town," Ginny noted. "If it is real, it must have come with the carnival."

"It's a long shot, but what if the cat saw something?" I said.

"Say you're right," Vinnie began and moved to unlock the holding cell door. "How do you propose we talk to it? It's a cat."

"I happen to have a telepathic chameleon who I know for a fact would be happy to help me translate," I answered. "But before we bring Beau into this, we need to talk to the tiger and its human partner from the show."

"Because ghosts can possess people if they are magical in life, but we have no idea if the carnival cast is supernatural," Ginny said, her cheeks flushing with the barest hint of embarrassment. She still felt guilty over what had happened at Halloween.

"Right. I still need to take Rick's statement and determine a way to plausibly rule him out as a suspect before I head back to the carnival."

"No, deputy, you need a shower and food," Rick answered and handed him the food and coffee Ginny had brought for him.

"Yes, sir." Vinnie took it without argument. Rick remained seated in the cell.

"Come back when you've cleaned up. I promise, I'm not going anywhere."

"I'll come back with something for you," Ginny offered and Rick nodded his agreement.

"Then I guess we're headed back to the carnival," Maggie noted, looping her arm through mine.

I reached out a hand to stop Ginny from leaving. "Ginny, on your way back, could you swing by the B&B and ask Tania to have Beau meet us on the carnival grounds? Just in case we run into the cat."

"Sure."

I didn't relish the idea of confronting someone who could change into a tiger about the death of the man who was technically their boss, but we needed to prove that Rick wasn't the actual killer. We walked back down Main Street and to Tyson's property. The carnival staff still milled about, but they didn't appear to be manning stalls or rides just yet.

I spotted Tessa among the staff, directing people around. She spotted Maggie and I, moving to intercept us. "Did the police arrest that man?"

"That man is the Chief of Police," I answered. "He's being questioned. But we were actually hoping you might be able to tell us about one of the other acts from last night?"

"I guess."

"The man with the tiger—" I began.

"Louis and Marcus," she filled in.

"Right. Well, I don't want to go accusing anyone of things they haven't done, but I mean, you have a tiger in your troupe. And it looked like Silvan was mauled."

"Marcus wouldn't hurt a fly," she protested.

"Is he a shapeshifter?" Maggie asked.

"Well, uh ... yes."

"And does he like being a shapeshifter?"

Tessa shrugged. "You'd have to ask him. But I'm telling you, he wouldn't hurt anyone. He's a gentle soul."

"Even the gentlest of souls can be provoked," I noted. "Please, we just want to talk to him. Could you point us to where we might find him?"

"Their trailer is back behind the Ferris Wheel. The one with the red curtains."

"Thank you," I said and led the way towards the rides. The Ferris Wheel loomed in the sky ahead of us.

We wound our way around the mechanism of the ride and back behind a row of trailers. They looked remarkably like the one Silvan had died behind. As we moved down the row toward the one at the end—the one with the red curtains—I spotted something shoved behind the steps to one of the closer trailers. I bent down, pulling out a pair of pants and shirt.

"This looks like what Rick was wearing yesterday," I said, holding it up for Maggie to see.

"Yes, it does." Maggie pulled out her phone and tapped away the screen. "Leave them, I just let Vinnie to know where they are. He'll come collect them for additional evidence."

A shiver danced down my spine as we continued down the row to the trailer at the end with the red curtains. That same sense of foreboding returned as I knocked on the door. A muscular man with a mop of reddish-brown hair answered.

"I've been waiting for someone to come talk to me. You better come inside."

9

The way he invited us in, as if he'd been expecting us, made me nervous. We hadn't told anyone else from the carnival except for Tessa that we were headed this way. And I didn't think tigers could hear quite that far, especially when in human form. Maggie nudged my shoulder, and I took an awkward step forward into the trailer.

I wasn't sure what I expected to find inside, but it wasn't the pristine interior. The two chairs on either side of a small dining table were sleek dark wood, almost like cherry, matched the table's gleaming surface. On the other end of the space sat a love seat with thick, burgundy-colored cushions. Matching drapes hung from the window by the dining table. Marcus watched us as Maggie and I stood on the threshold. His eyes were kind if a bit inquisitive. I could make out a strange hint of green ringing his irises, not unlike the amber flecks that signaled Chief Hayes was more than he appeared.

"Can I get you something to drink? Coffee or water?" Marcus' voice broke the silence as if it had been a physical barrier between us.

"I'm fine, thanks. Uh, not that we don't appreciate the hospitality, but why'd you say you were expecting someone to come around to talk to you?" I took a step towards the love seat, but Marcus directed us towards the hardwood chairs around the table.

He gave me a sad smile. "I gave a statement to that poor overworked policeman last night, but everything was so chaotic I figured he would need to follow up. So, he sent you two."

"We aren't police," Maggie corrected him.

"Could have fooled me," he snorted. "I saw you at the ... scene, too."

"We found Silvan's body," I explained.

Marcus shook his head. "No one should die like that. No one should be alone like that in death."

Before I could respond, Maggie squeezed my arm and pulled me around, so we no longer faced

Marcus. She leaned in, her lips brushing my earlobe. "We have to ask him about his alibi."

"Surely Vinnie's done that already."

"Vinnie probably wouldn't put it together about Marcus being a shapeshifter and I doubt a shifter would volunteer the information to someone he perceives as mundane." After a sharp breath, she added, "Besides, he wouldn't be the first potential suspect you've questioned."

She wasn't wrong. I'd interviewed my fair share of people who were mighty suspicious in town over the last few years. Whether I'd intended to take on the role or not. And I still owed it to Rick to find the truth about what happened, even if we knew he wasn't the one responsible now.

"We aren't here on behalf of the police, but we were hoping to ask you some questions about your time with the carnival," I noted, pivoting to face him again. I took the seat he'd indicated. Maggie moved to stand behind me. I could feel her fingertips brush my shoulders in a show of support.

Marcus looked at the small hot plate in the corner where a single serving teakettle sat on top. "I'll answer whatever you want to know, but I really think some coffee would be in order."

"We're fine, really," Maggie answered. "But, if you feel more relaxed with a cup, don't let us stop you."

My stomach did a nervous flip as he set about preparing some instant coffee in the kettle. I suppose he had to make do with what he had. Still, given how much the carnival appeared to bring in with sales, I would have assumed they'd all have a better set up. Most modern mobile homes were fully equipped with at least a kitchen.

"We noticed some clothes on the ground not far from here, they don't belong to you, do they?" I began, resting my elbows on the edge of the table.

"Clothes? I don't think so. We always change in the stalls behind the big top."

I hadn't noticed any stalls when we'd gone looking for Silvan, but then again, I'd been otherwise engaged. "Look, I don't want to come off as rude or blunt, but we know you can change form. You're the tiger from last night's act, right?"

Marcus stopped fiddling with the kettle and looked at us. "I don't hide it."

"I'm honestly surprised you don't. I would imagine it could be a rather scary thing for people to learn when they first meet you," Maggie offered.

"I don't usually go around telling townies about it. But the rest of us in the show, we've been together long enough that we don't keep secrets from each other."

"It's also no secret that it looked like Silvan was mauled by something with pretty sharp claws," I continued, fixing him with a pointed expression.

Marcus instinctively looked down at his hands, studying his nails as if he were inspecting a recently done manicure. "It wasn't me."

"Can you think of anyone else who might have wanted to hurt Silvan?" I pressed.

"No. He was a tough man to live with sometimes, but he was what kept us together after ... " he trailed off.

"After your old ringmaster died?"

He nodded. "We owed him for that."

"How exactly were they related?"

"Cousins."

"I've seen a photo of the former proprietor, and I wouldn't exactly say they looked like cousins. They looked like they could be identical twins."

"Strong family genetics. Look, I didn't hurt him. After our act, Louis and I came back here to unwind. The show works us both up, and we needed to blow off some steam."

"And you're sure you didn't see anyone come by before the murder?"

Marcus' cheeks flushed. "I wasn't exactly paying attention to what was happening outside, if you know what I mean."

"And there's no one else who could have attacked him? No one else with claws?"

Marcus shook his head. "No."

So much for this conversation giving us a fresh suspect. In the back of my mind, I recalled that Beau was on his way. Maybe we could track down the strange ghostly cat and have a chat with it. Then again, getting into Silvan's trailer was worth a shot, too.

"We have a friend who is like you ... well not exactly like you, but he was forcibly changed the last time the carnival came through town," Maggie interjected. "Mind explaining how that happened?"

"I only joined the carnival about six years ago. Anything before that I wouldn't know about." Behind him, the kettle burbled as water heated for his instant coffee.

"When you joined the carnival, were you already like this? Could you already change into a tiger?" I continued Maggie's line of questioning.

"It's why they accepted me. I'd met Louis a few times on the road, and I fell in love, hard. He was so funny and genuine that I knew I had to be with him. But he warned me that the carnival wasn't for the faint of heart and you had to really be something special to join. When I auditioned, well it became clear pretty fast that they needed another creature act, and I figured I could fill that void. The fact I got to do it with the man I loved made it even better."

"So, no one made you this way?" I pressed, trying to grasp exactly how one could become a shapeshifter.

Marcus went quiet again, averting his gaze. "Outside of your traditional wolves, the rest of us are created with magic. Transmogrification spells, mostly."

"Could that be what happened to our friend?" Maggie pressed.

"I honestly can't say."

"And you're positive you're the only other wild creature in the carnival?" I leaned in closer, wishing I had Ginny at my side to compel the truth from his mouth. I couldn't shake the sense he was holding something back.

"As far as I know, yes. But this town has a reputation for the supernatural, too. It could have come from within your own community."

I didn't like his suggestion, especially since we'd

found enough evidence to clear Rick as a suspect. Still, I held my tongue.

"You and your husband don't do much in the way of acts outside the big top, right?" Maggie probed.

"That's right. Why?"

"Well, it just seems a little strange that you're here, but he's not."

I'd been so focused on trying to learn what Marcus might know about Silvan's death, I hadn't even stopped to consider that his human partner was missing in action.

"He's been helping Tessa keep things from falling apart. Trying to keep morale up. He left early this morning."

I filed that away as something to look into later. "If you think of anything else or hear something that might help, you should tell the police," I prompted before standing up.

"Can't think of what else I'd know, but ... " Marcus trailed off, his gaze narrowing at a spot off on left shoulder. "Sorry, did you know you've got a hitch-hiker that just appeared?"

I felt the subtle digging of Beau's claws into my shoulder; not enough to hurt, just to give me a hint that he was present. I was more surprised by the fact he hadn't felt the need to camouflage himself in front of Marcus. It wasn't like my reptilian companion to simply reveal himself during an investigation.

"Beau's not a hitchhiker, he's a friend," I answered and pushed myself to my feet. "But his arrival does remind me that we've got to get going."

Marcus nodded wordlessly, watching as Maggie and I left the trailer behind. I exhaled an audible breath once the door shut behind us. "That felt like we were going in circles," I groaned as we put distance between us and Marcus.

"Well, we know that Silvan probably didn't turn him into a tiger. And he does genuinely seem to enjoy being part of the carnival. But it is suspicious he didn't see or hear more."

"Well, I suppose we should see if we can find that spectral cat that keeps giving Sam the shivers," I said.

"We still don't have any real sense why anyone would want Silvan dead," Maggie pointed out.

"I mean, he was a smarmy showman. He clearly had enemies, even if Rick didn't do it. There's something off about the way he took over the carnival. We need to get into Silvan's trailer and take a look around."

"Good thing we've got someone who can make us

invisible, then," Maggie said with a smirk and petted Beau's head.

"What do you think, mate? You up for a little light snooping?" I couldn't see the reptile on my shoulder, but I felt the ripple of his magic enveloping me and took that as answer enough.

Maggie looped her fingers through mine. Together we walked quickly and as silently as possible across the grounds to Silvan's trailer. The strands of crime scene tape still rippled in the breeze behind the structure. It felt eerie sneaking into a dead man's inner sanctum, but if we were going to get any sort of answers, it was where we needed to look. I balled my hand into the hem of my shirt to avoid leaving fingerprints and pulled the handle on the trailer's front door.

It opened outward on squeaky hinges, and I held my breath, pausing mid-motion as I waited for someone to notice our entry. No one came running and nothing jumped out at us for daring to enter. I exhaled again and eased the door the rest of the way open. I felt Maggie's hand leave mine and she walked up the three steps of the stairs inside. I followed her, pulling the door shut behind me.

The trailer was almost in pristine condition. There was a small kitchenette on the far back wall, attached to what looked like a toilet and perhaps a single stall shower. Far fancier than Marcus and Louis' accommodations. The stove boasted two gas burners which shone in the early morning sunlight. Nothing appeared out of place, not even the pillows on the bed were a fraction out of alignment.

"So, he was a neat freak?" I whispered.

"He certainly liked things to be organized," Maggie agreed and crept towards the back of the trailer to the bathroom.

I turned my attention to the space that boasted a small table with two chairs and a tiny chest of drawers nestled into one corner. It looked to be a custom build as the drawers were narrower than any I'd seen before. I took a quick peek through the cabinets—finding nothing but a couple sets of dishes and mugs neatly organized in size order. Nothing to suggest why anyone would brutally maul the carnival owner to death.

'Drawers'

"I know, I know," I murmured under my breath to Beau as I shut the cabinets. I could hear Maggie still rummaging through things at the other end of the trailer. So, I focused my attention on the tiny drawers nestled into the corner between the sink and the exterior wall. I bent down and tried the handle on the top drawer. It stuck a little, but after I gave it a firm yank, it came free. A small black leatherbound book with a silver clasp was tucked inside. If Vinnie hadn't found it already, he wouldn't miss it. I set it on the table behind me and tried the second drawer.

This one turned out to be deeper than the first and opened more freely. Inside sat a single framed photograph lying face down at the bottom of the drawer. I plucked the frame free and turned the photo right side up. Silvan and Tessa looked at each other with the glittering lights of the carnival behind them. He wore what looked to be a tuxedo and top hat. She was in an elegant, curve hugging white dress.

"Uh, Maggie. I think you should see this," I called.

I heard clattering from the tiny bathroom and Maggie appeared holding a collection of bottles, some with vibrantly colored liquids inside while others held bits of herbs. "I think I found something, too."

"Silvan or whatever name he used to go by is married to Tessa," I announced, holding up the picture frame. "Or at least she used to be."

"That would give someone a motive for murder all right, especially if things soured between them in the interim," Maggie agreed. "I'm not totally sure, but these ingredients could be used in advanced spell work. Like serious potions."

"The kind that could turn someone into an animal?"

"Possibly. I'd need to figure out what exactly these are, but the idea doesn't give me warm and fuzzy feelings."

I scooped up the leather clad book and shoved it into the hem of my pants. "I think we should keep this somewhere safe until we know more."

I snapped a photo of the wedding picture and placed it back in the drawer. Things were getting stranger and stranger, and we were no closer to finding answers than when we'd started the day.

10

We made it halfway down the thoroughfare before I felt Beau's tiny claws dig into my shoulder in warning. I stopped walking, used my arm to stop Maggie, and glanced about, worried someone had spotted us coming out of Silvan's trailer. Beau had dropped his invisibility once we were clear and I hadn't noticed anyone else around, but that didn't mean we'd gotten away unseen.

"What do you see?" My words came out in a whisper.

'Company. Around the corner.'

I felt Beau's weight shift slightly and his head bobbed off to our left. I craned my neck in hopes of spotting the aforementioned company, but saw no one. And then, like a mirage, the spectral cat I'd spotted in the rafters appeared at ground level. It's large tail flicked behind it and our gazes met. It was unnerving the way the creature seemed to look straight through me.

'*Follow him.*'

Yes, this had been the whole reason we'd sent for Beau in the first place. We needed to have a chat with the ghost. So, as the feline darted away from the carnival, I followed, doing my best to keep it's translucent form in view. Maggie hurried beside me, not asking for an explanation. The cat continued on its path away from the noise of the carnival grounds to the quieter stretch of Main Street. It stopped just outside Ginny's cafe, looking back at me as if expecting me to open the door for it.

Well, that seemed odd, given what I knew about ghosts and their ability to pass through solid barriers such as doors and walls. I peered through the front window. The establishment was sparsely populated. I supposed it was as good a place as any to have this little chat.

So, I opened the door, allowing the cat to dart inside. In short order, it leapt into the seat at one of the back booths. At least it understood discretion. I moved to sit opposite the creature, and Maggie followed, sliding into the booth beside me.

"Uh, maybe get us a couple of coffees, so the servers don't come over thinking we're talking to thin air?" I suggested when Maggie fixed me with a 'what now?' expression.

"Good idea. Don't get to the juicy details before I'm back though."

The cat stared me down while I waited for Maggie to return. Beau dislodged himself from my shoulder and moved to blend in with the table in front of us. His tail hung over the edge, a hint of green to it still, so Maggie didn't accidentally try to put down the coffee mugs where he'd settled. She returned a moment later with two mugs. I took a fortifying sip before I turned my full attention to the ghost opposite of us.

"Um, I'm not really sure how this is meant to work. Do you understand what I'm saying?"

The cat, which up close did in fact look like a lynx, tilted its head to one side and fixed its eerie yellow gaze on the spot Beau had claimed.

'Yes, he understands and is male.'

I looked at Maggie. "Beau says the cat understands and apparently, is a he."

"Guess we better start asking our questions."

"I don't want to be impolite, so what should I call you?"

'GhostCat,' came Beau's voice in my head.

"Ghost cat?"

'One word.'

It seemed a bit on the nose, but who I was to argue with a sentient feline ghost. "Thanks for explaining Beau. GhostCat, do you know what happened to Silvan, the man who runs the carnival?"

GhostCat licked his lips, his pale pink tongue darting out and in again. He blinked once and bobbed his head, almost as if to say 'yes.' But I waited for Beau's translation.

'He was killed.'

"Did you see how it happened? I know you were in the big top before, but you disappeared."

The ghost sniffed at one of his large paws dismissively.

'Didn't see.'

Of course he didn't. That would have been far too convenient. Even if it meant having to come up with a creative way to present the evidence to Vinnie and Rick, a small part of me had hoped the spectral cat would have held the answers we were looking for.

"Is there anything you do know? You can't have been watching me and Sam for no reason."

There was a prolonged wait for Beau to translate. I hoped that meant he was trying to synthesize a lot of useful information.

'Silvan dangerous. A deceiver.'

"Yeah, no offense but we already knew that. He changed his name a few years ago and thinks no one noticed."

'Look at why.'

"We will. But why show yourself to Sam and me?"

GhostCat bared his sharp teeth at us and stood.

'Because he can.'

There wasn't a more cat answer than that. Without warning, GhostCat darted to the floor and made for the doorway as someone unknowingly opened it. Just as the ghost crossed the threshold, it looked back at us. I could swear it almost smiled.

'Tessa knows.'

With that, GhostCat vanished out of sight. I slumped against the booth and rubbed at my temples. "She knows what?" I mumbled, not expecting a response.

"She who?" Maggie prompted.

"Tessa. The last thing he said before he took off was Tessa knows. But she knows what?"

"Well, it seems pretty clear that she and Silvan are or were married at one time. We should look into that. Maybe there's divorce records somewhere?"

"Maybe. But as far as I could tell, whatever her powers were related to being really agile in the air."

Maggie's brow furrowed. "When you were using your magic to see the crime happening, there was that strange rippling over the grass. Could she have been levitating?"

"Maybe."

"He also said that Silvan was dangerous and a deceiver."

"Why don't we head back to my place? I can dig into what he might have been cooking up with those bottles of herbs and liquids. You could see what you can find about him and Tessa."

She was right. We had more digging to do before we could bring anything to Vinnie and Rick. As if summoned by the mere thought of him, Vinnie walked through the door, stopping at the counter only long enough to pick up an extra-large to-go coffee cup and a small, wrapped sandwich. He spotted Maggie and I and after a moment of hesitation, he joined us in the booth.

"You two look positively conspiratorial," he said with a tired smile.

"We've just had a rather strange conversation with a ghost," I explained. "He didn't think very highly of Silvan, and he thinks Tessa knows something."

"She did step up and take the reins on the whole operation pretty fast," he noted.

"We're seeing what we might be able to find through publicly available information," I offered.

"I appreciate it. Because honestly, I'm still stumped. I know it wasn't Rick who attacked him. Yet the wounds do appear to have been made by a large animal."

"We chatted with Marcus, the bloke who can turn into a tiger. He claimed he had an alibi corroborated by his husband."

Vinnie's brow knit together in thought. "I think I remember talking to them. They were in their trailer ..." He cleared his throat. "Anyway, I didn't see any obvious evidence they were involved."

"One thing I did notice was how his husband wasn't around during our chat. I haven't seen any of the performers or vendors in town, so he's got to be on the carnival grounds somewhere." I made the last comment to assuage my own nerves as much as assure Vinnie he didn't need to worry about going after a missing potential witness.

"You didn't happen to find anything else while you were, uh ... exploring the grounds?" Vinnie chose his words carefully.

"I don't know what you mean," I protested.

"Darcy, come on. We all know you went back there. It's how you figured out what really happened with Rick."

"Well, it felt like maybe someone else was there. And Tessa seems to be able to levitate. So, maybe that's what GhostCat meant by 'Tessa knows.' Maybe she happened upon the murder and is scared of whoever the killer is?"

"Sounds like I need to have another chat with her."

"Give us a little time to figure out what we can about her history with Silvan ... or who he used to be first," Maggie interjected. "You want all the ammunition you can find before you bring her in and start accusing her of withholding information."

"I can give you an hour, maybe two. But I honestly don't think any of people with the carnival want to stick around any longer than they have to. And no one is outright saying they're worried about the town's safety, but I can feel the unease as people walk by the grounds," Vinnie answered.

"Then let us see what we can dig up," I said,

downing the rest of my coffee and nudging Maggie's shoulder for her to let me out of the booth. Before I had a chance to stand, I felt the light pressure of Beau crawling up my arm and settling on my right shoulder. He rippled momentarily into existence before he took on the matching hues of my top and vanished again. Vinnie made no comment as he, too, got to his feet and reclaimed his to-go cup and sandwich.

The three of us left Ginny's behind and split off as Vinnie started back towards the police station. Maggie and I returned to her flat and settled in the living room. She set me up with her laptop and I stared at the screen in a bit of decision paralysis.

"We have no idea where they're even from, so looking in local databases seems silly," I said when Maggie fixed me with a 'what's wrong' expression.

"Maybe start with news articles about what supposedly happened to Silvan's cousin?"

I did a search for the carnival plus the keywords 'death' and 'suspicious,' but nothing came up. What had Rick said Silvan's name had been before? Gregor something? I tried putting in 'carnival death Gregor.' A brief article from a small newspaper in Maine came up in the search results from five years ago.

Enigmatic Carnival Leader Presumed Dead

By: Tori Sinclair

Late Saturday, reports came in that Ivan Gregor, owner of a traveling supernatural carnival, vanished from the grounds of his latest stop. Witnesses reported seeing evidence of a fire being set on the premises. No word on if a body was ever found. Speculation abounds about what could have prompted the fire and if the charismatic showman really did perish.

One witness who spoke under the condition of anonymity stated they swore Gregor had set the blaze himself outside one of the travel trailers. A woman who appeared to be part of the cast was seen nearby as well. The investigation is ongoing, but members of the carnival report that they heard Gregor arguing with his wife shortly before the fire started.

"Well, it looks like Tessa and Ivan, Silvan's prior alias were married at least at the time he supposedly died in a fire."

"Supposedly?"

"Well, no one seems to know if he actually died or not. At the very least a body was never found. And according to this article, some people saw Tessa near the fire, too. And she and Gregor might have fought beforehand."

"That definitely sounds suspect," Maggie agreed.

"We don't know what sort of magic Silvan ... or Ivan, or whatever you want to call him, had."

"Well, I'd guess it had something to do with transmogrification like Marcus said," Maggie answered. "He might not have been the one to turn Marcus, but we know for a fact he turned Rick. And he's got the ability to compel people to do what he wants."

"Could he have more than one ability?"

"I mean, I haven't heard of a witch having more than one ability before, but I suppose it's possible. What are you thinking?"

"Well, when he was running the show the night he died, a sense came over me, like I couldn't look away. He drew me in, compelling me. The article even called him charismatic, but what if it's more than that? What if he can influence people? Change their perception? It could explain how he got the whole carnival to believe he was a completely different person."

"I think you're right." Maggie held up some of the vials and jars she'd taken from Silvan's trailer. "These definitely seem like they could cause a change in someone's physiology. But as long as you had some ounce of magic in you, with enough practice, you could do it. It's not an innate ability though, more a perversion of nature, honestly."

"It still feels like we're missing a piece of the puzzle. Why would he be doing it in the first place? Surely there's enough magical people in the country he could find someone who wanted to live out their dreams as a performer rather than force them?"

Maggie shrugged. "Maybe he just liked big cats? They are more impressive as an act than just human beings doing extraordinary things. There could be hidden wires or harnesses involved with people and attendees might try to look for the trick. But a wild animal, they know that takes skill to tame them."

I hated her logic, but I couldn't argue with it. "We need to have another chat with Tessa before Vinnie brings her in. Maybe we can get her to open up and give us something we can use to figure out if she was involved, or at least find out what she knows?"

"Just be careful, Darcy. Like you said, she could have been involved in setting a fire to try and kill her husband once before."

"I wasn't planning to go alone," I noted hopefully.

"Not that I want you to head back there solo, I do have to get to work." She gestured to the bottles still sitting on the counter. "And I'd like some more time with this stuff. See if I can figure out exactly how he did what he did."

I picked up on an unspoken addition to Maggie's words, the hope of reversing the effects.

"I'll see if Tania can come with me. Maybe she can pick up on Tessa's emotions faster and help guide the conversation."

"Good idea. I'll call you as soon as I figure out anything else. You do the same?"

I set the laptop aside and moved to stand across from her. "Of course." I gave her a swift kiss before leaving her flat. I made it to street level just in time to see Tania hurrying towards me.

"You told her, didn't you?" I asked the reptile still perched on my shoulder.

'Protect my friends.'

"Cheers, mate. Why don't you go keep Maggie company." The chameleon blinked at me lazily before disappearing, his familiar weight vanishing from my shoulder.

"So, Beau says you need my help questioning someone?" Tania sounded surprisingly excited by the prospect.

"Yes, a possible witness. Or a potential killer."

"Then we'd best be careful. I will do what I can to keep things even keeled."

Together we retraced the route down Main Street towards the edge of town. I couldn't shake the sense of unease settling over me that we were about to walk into more than just a friendly chat.

11

 did my best to fill Tania in on what Maggie and I had discovered so far, including the history between Tessa and Ivan, GhostCat's warning that Tessa knew something and that Silvan had been a deceiver. And the fact that Marcus' husband hadn't been spotted since Vinnie took their statements.

"Maggie thinks she might be able to create some sort of antidote." Tania posed as the carnival grounds and the very back of Tyson's shop came into view.

"That would be my guess. I mean, if we have a chance to give Rick that peace of mind back, to help heal his trauma, don't we have to try?"

"Yes, of course. I just worry she is taking on too

much. That sort of magic can be quite advanced and dangerous if done incorrectly."

"If there's anyone who can figure it out, it's her. Besides, she's got loads of experience with potions and tinctures as a healer. This can't be that different."

Tania made a noncommittal noise that signaled she still didn't agree, but wasn't going to push it anymore. Even though Maggie and I had been on the grounds only a short while ago, the atmosphere had shifted dramatically. Where before the carnival workers had been milling about, restocking their stalls, now they'd all vanished from sight. A chill rand down my spine as we stepped through the still-open front gates. The space was too quiet for all of the life that had filled it only a short while ago.

"This feels off," I said, moving closer to Tania.

"There is a lot of fear in this place," Tania replied, reaching down to grip my hand in hers. "And grief. But ... not about the death exactly."

"How do you mean?"

"It's as if ... they are mourning the lives they had lived until now."

"We'd thought Silvan ... or Ivan could manipulate or control perception and emotions. Maybe whatever he did to fake his death five years ago is fading since he's actually died?"

"That might explain it." She looked around and gave my hand another squeeze. "Where would we find Tessa?"

"I honestly haven't a clue. I talked to her here the first day and then I saw her when she came around the back to find the body that night. But I don't know which trailer is hers."

"Are we certain she wasn't sharing one with Silvan? If he had been her husband maybe they were actually still together?"

"I got the sense they weren't together. When I brought up Ivan, she got this sort of faraway look and the short time I saw them interacting there was nothing like an intimate relationship. They appeared all business."

"Then I suppose we should start going one by one until we find her or ask someone who can tell us where to go."

We moved past the row of stalls across from the looming Ferris Wheel and beyond the big top. I spotted Marcus and Louis' trailer still where it sat before. Only this time, the interior looked unoccupied and the trailers on either side of it were equally dark. I took another step forward and nearly lost my footing when GhostCat materialized blocking my way. I didn't think I'd harm the ghost by stepping through him, but having done so with Sam in the past, I knew it was unpleasant for all involved.

"I'm sorry, I don't have Beau with me. But we're trying to find Tessa. You said she knows something? Can you help us find her?"

GhostCat paced in front of me, the tips of his ears flicking in time to the movement. He said nothing—not that I could have understood him without Beau's assistance—but he appeared agitated. I looked at Tania. "Can you get anything from him?"

"Agitation. Worry. Rather human emotions for a cat."

GhostCat flicked his tail, let out a silent yowl and took off away from the trailers towards Tyson's shop. Without thinking, I followed him. I heard the sound of Tania's shoes slapping against the ground behind me. I didn't stop to make sure she kept up. I couldn't risk losing sight of the spectral lynx. He darted around the front of Tyson's shop just in time for me to see Tyson shove a tall figure out the front door.

"Come into my establishment again peddling things that don't belong to you, and I'll have you arrested!"

The man who stepped into the mid-morning light looked like the man I'd seen opposite of

Marcus' tiger form the night before. So, Louis had stuck around after all. But what was he trying to sell that wasn't his? He noticed me looking at him, shoved his hands into his pockets, and started off around the other side of the shop.

"Wait a minute!" I called, rushing after the man. "Can I just ask you one question?"

"You're with the locals," he replied.

"I'm just looking for Tessa, that's all."

He halted, but didn't turn to face me. "What for?"

"She seemed pretty upset and I can't blame her, finding the body of someone she'd spent so much time with. I wanted to check on her. Besides, she stepped up to run things and that's got to be a lot of pressure out of the blue."

"I don't know where she is," he answered.

"Could you at least tell me which trailer is hers?"

He gave a heavy sigh and pointed with his left hand. "Last one on the right."

I spotted something small and glittery clutched in his hand. Likely whatever he'd been trying to pawn Tyson. Without another word, Louis shoved his hands into his pockets and hurried off. I retreated to the front door of Tyson's shop where he still stood with Tania. GhostCat had slunk away again, but at least he had helped us answer the question of Louis' whereabouts.

"What was he trying to sell you?" I addressed the shop owner.

"He tried to sell me jewelry that was clearly not his."

"How could you tell?" I realized the stupidity of my question the moment I'd asked it. Of course, Tyson could tell it didn't belong to Louis. That was the entire point of the spell Ginny had cast over the shop in the first place. "Sorry, never mind."

Tyson gave me a small smile. "I didn't need magic to tell it wasn't his. For one thing, there was blood on it. He clearly thought he'd cleaned it off, but it was there. And the way he kept looking over his shoulder, like he thought someone was going to see what he was doing didn't help convince me he was innocent."

"What type of jewelry was he trying to sell you?" Tania interjected.

"It was a pendant. A locket really. He didn't open it, but he had the gall to tell me it belonged to his mother. But the style is much too modern."

Having stolen property covered in blood wasn't a good look for Louis, but I still couldn't understand why he would attack Silvan. "You must hear things from the performers and the rest of the carnival workers while they're around or passing by the shop. Has anyone said anything strange since Silvan's death? Like maybe they're not broken up about it?" I failed to hide the hint of hopefulness in my tone.

"I can tell you that man and his husband aren't as happy as they want you to believe," Tyson answered. "Before the show yesterday, they were outside talking. I'm sure they didn't think anyone heard them because of all the excitement happening in the big top. But I came back in to check on a few things and I heard them arguing. Mister Sticky Fingers said he was tired of their act always being on the roster."

"I could understand that. I mean I can't imagine it's particularly comfortable for Marcus to have to shift form all the time," Tania said.

"Enough to want to kill a man? And I've already talked to Marcus. So has Vinnie. There isn't any evidence he did it."

"Did you ask him to get his claws out?" Tyson snorted.

"Well ... no."

"We came to talk to Tessa, not speculate about a man Vinnie already cleared," Tania reminded me.

Tyson wasn't wrong to point out I hadn't really checked Marcus for evidence, and I doubted Vinnie had swabbed for DNA under his tiger claws. Tyson stepped back into the darkened interior of his shop as we headed to the row of trailers and the one Louis had pointed out.

On the way, I dialed Ginny's number, my nerves jangling as I waited for her to pick up. She answered on the second ring.

"Did you find something that could help Vinnie?"

"Maybe. But I was kind of hoping you might be able to help me with something. It shouldn't' take long."

"What?"

"Could you do a quick online search for any photos you can find of Silvan or Tessa? Promotional shots, maybe candid pictures where they're in the background."

"What should I be looking for?"

"A locket. Probably gold."

"I will see what I can do." I heard something whistling in the background. "Give me a few minutes and I'll text you anything I find."

"You're a lifesaver. Thank you."

Stowing my phone in my pocket, I marched on towards the end of the row of trailers. Tania kept pace with me, hands swinging loosely at her sides.

"Have you thought about what you're going to say to Tessa to get her to divulge her secrets to you?"

"Just hoping a friendly face might loosen her lips."

"Ever the optimist," she noted softly.

We approached the last trailer on the right to find the door ajar. I spotted GhostCat sitting in the window, eyeing me expectantly. Its yellow eyes glowed almost like lamp lights in the darkened interior. I felt Tania's hand on my wrist, trying to pull me back from entering. The cat had been guiding us towards Tessa since we'd crossed paths earlier.

"It looks like no one is in there," I whispered.

"That doesn't mean we should go in."

"I'll be quick."

I pushed the door inward with the side of my foot and stepped into the trailer. It looked remarkably similar to the one Marcus and Louis shared. Except the inside was in complete disarray. Clothes were strewn about the floor, and I spotted some broken dishes gathered up in the sink. A few shards still littered the floor. I had no sense of whether this had been Tessa's doing—perhaps the memory of being married to Silvan in his prior persona overwhelming her with grief—or maybe anger had simply bubbled over at being used and left to fend for herself?

"You want to help me out here?" I addressed the lynx still lounging by the front window. He fixed me with a feline look of superiority before slinking down and meandering his way to the far end of the trailer where a single bed sat up against one wall.

The damage to what might be considered the bedroom was even more extensive. Glass from picture frames glittered over multiple surfaces and I thought I could spy a few flecks of blood amongst them. The pictures themselves lay torn in pieces on the pillow. My heart hammered as I carefully picked one up, using the hem of my shirt as a barrier. The same photo I'd found in Silvan's drawer had been mangled and spots appeared to have recent burn marks where Silvan's face had been.

This scene certainly appeared as though Tessa was overcome with memories about what she'd already lost once when the man who I assumed had professed his love for her, made her forget who he was. I still didn't understand what would have driven him to such an act.

"Darcy, someone's coming," Tania called.

I let the photo fragments fall back to the bed

before retreating to the front door. I hurried back to the entrance to leave the space behind. When I reached it, Tania grabbed my arm and pulled me away without saying another word. She didn't let go until we were back behind the stalls on the main thoroughfare.

"Who was it?" I asked, trying to catch my breath.

"I don't know, but whoever it was, I could sense their anger. We did not need to be there when they arrived."

Before I could respond, my phone rang with an incoming call from the police station. I couldn't lie I was disappointed Ginny hadn't gotten back to me yet. Still, the bottom dropped out of my stomach as I answered it, wondering why Vinnie or Rick hadn't simply called me from their mobile. "This is Darcy."

"Darcy, it's Vinnie," the deputy said on the other end of the line.

"Everything okay? You're calling from the station."

"Where are you right now?" I picked up on the panic in his tone.

"Still down at the carnival grounds. What's going on? You're worrying me."

"Well, we've gotten some additional forensics

back and it looks like there was a second person involved. Silvan's cause of death wasn't from the wounds in his chest. Not entirely anyway. His larynx was crushed. Someone suffocated him."

12

The worry in Vinnie's voice stuck with me as Tania and I wound our way through the carnival grounds. The tension between my shoulder blades eased only once we were firmly on the sidewalk of Main Street heading in the direction of the police station.

"What did you find inside?" Tania kept glancing over her shoulder.

"Someone trashed the place. I'm not sure when exactly, but I found some ripped up photographs of Tessa and Silvan, or I suppose he was Ivan back then. It felt like someone had just let out all of their pent-up rage."

"So, she likely wasn't attacked."

"I'm no expert, but I didn't get that feeling." I

glanced at my landlady. "Did you pick up on anything?"

"Sometimes places can give off emotional imprints if there has been significant and recent trauma, but I did not sense anything like that from where I stood."

I stopped when we reached the front entrance to the police station and looked back the way we'd come. For a brief moment, I could swear I spotted Ghost-Cat's spectral form trailing us. Maybe he was just making sure we'd got out safely? Before I could decide on my next move, the front doors whooshed open and Vinnie appeared, practically grabbing my forearm.

His cheeks were still pale, obviously the coffee and sandwich he'd had earlier did little to help his pallor. If anything, the caffeine had only made the man more jittery. He ushered Tania inside as well before leading us back into Rick's office.

"Vinnie, maybe you should take a break?" I suggested when we'd all crammed into the space around Rick's desk.

"I can't, not when the people in this town are in danger," he retorted.

"You have been at this for far too long without sleep. Darcy is right, you need to take care of yourself. Otherwise, you can't take care of the people in this town," Tania said kindly.

"I've been telling him the same thing since he let me out of holding," Rick muttered. "Think I instilled too much of a work ethic in him early on."

"You said something about evidence showing someone else was there when Silvan died. That the wounds in his chest didn't kill him?"

Vinnie shuffled through some photographs and pointed to some faint bruising on Silvan's neck. "It looks like someone stepped on his throat to stop him from breathing."

Someone who could move around without leaving footprints.

"And you think it might be Tessa?"

"We all saw the high wire act. Performers with magic are in the show for a reason."

"I don't disagree, but we didn't get a chance to talk to her." After a beat I added, "We did run into Louis trying to pawn what we surmised was a stolen locket to Tyson."

"Bet that went over swimmingly," Rick snorted.

"Well, there was blood on it," Tania offered. "And Tyson heard him and his husband arguing before the show last night."

"So, we've got two potential killers," I said. "Or did they just decide to team up?"

"It seems as though there are more questions that need to be answered in order to make that assessment," Tania noted.

"Do you have any idea where Tessa might have gone?" Rick addressed me, his gaze sharp and inquisitive. Clearly, he had taken time to rest and was back to his usual self.

That alone made me feel a little better about the whole situation.

"Well, she wasn't in her trailer when we went looking for her just now. But the place was a mess. It looked like she'd trashed it herself. Also, we found a torn-up photo of her and Silvan ... or Ivan in the mess."

"What sort of photo?" Vinnie rubbed at the stubble on his chin.

"It was a wedding photo I think." I stopped short of admitting to snooping in Silvan's trailer. Since that would lead to confessing about involving Maggie and how we had borrowed the black leather book and the bottles of herbs with spell contents. They didn't need to know all of that until we knew more. "But it had been torn up and burned."

"But she can't change forms as far as we know.

So, how did he get mauled if she didn't do it?" Vinnie's question wasn't addressed to anyone in particular. "I found no evidence of blood or anything else that would have tied Marcus to the crime scene."

"Weren't you and Maggie working on that?" Tania gave me a pointed look.

Rick and Vinnie both zeroed in on me. *Ballocks, time to come clean.* "We sort of took a look through Silvan's trailer earlier. That's where I first saw a photo of him and Tessa. We found an article about a fire that supposedly killed Ivan five years ago. Some people thought she might have been involved. But the way she acted when I brought him up the first day of the carnival suggested she was under the same spell as everyone else. Like they all believed the ringmaster was a different person. I can't even say for sure that she remembered being married to him. Until maybe he died or was wounded?"

"What did Tania mean you were working on something?" Rick prodded.

"Oh, we found some odd herbs and tinctures too. Maggie thinks they might be partly how he managed to transform you. And possibly others. We didn't want to tell you until we knew more." Heat rose in my neck as I tried not to flinch under his intensifying gaze.

"Because you're trying to undo it."

"We aren't sure of anything yet and didn't think it was fair to get your hopes up."

"I'm a big boy. I can handle disappointment." Still, I detected a hint of desperation in his voice. "Right, well I think you two have done more than enough for this investigation. Given that we have potentially two dangerous people running around town, I think you'd be safer heading back and bunking down at the B&B."

"I know we aren't police, but this happened in our backyard," I protested. "People are more likely to talk to us, because we aren't police. Maybe we could get someone else to corroborate seeing Tessa or Louis near Silvan's trailer before he was killed?"

"I owe my freedom to you, Darcy. Those are not words I ever expected to say when I first met you. But you gave me my life back. But I can't, in good conscience, put you or your friends in harm's way. Let the professionals handle things from here on out."

I bit my tongue to keep from admitting I'd pulled his sister into the investigation, too. Things between them were still a touch icy from the whole booking-the-carnival-in-the-first-place thing. I didn't want to make things worse. But that didn't mean I couldn't have an early lunch and see what Ginny might have been able to find out. And there were still missing pieces I couldn't quite put my fingers on. Like what had prompted Ivan to fake his own death all those years ago?

"Did you get confirmation that Silvan and Ivan are one in the same?" I blurted before either Rick or Vinnie had the chance to usher me out of the room.

Vinnie glanced at a report that sat partially visible on Rick's desk. "Yes. We determined that his prints match those of Ivan Gregor. Doesn't mean he doesn't deserve answers though."

"You're right. Even if he was a prick in life, he still deserves the truth in death."

"I mean it, Darcy. You need to keep out of this from now on." Rick rounded the desk and opened the door. "And to make sure you get where you're supposed to be, I'm going to walk you there myself." To Vinnie he added, "Head back to the carnival grounds. See if you can track down any other witnesses or find Louis or Tessa themselves."

So much for Vinnie getting some rest.

Rick didn't give me any choice except to follow him out of the station, down Main Street, past Ginny's, and back to the front steps of the B&B. I expected Tanla to give him some grief about home confinement, but she said nothing. She simply went inside, leaving Rick and I alone on the front steps.

"If Maggie could reverse what Ivan did to you, would you want her to?" The words fell out of my mouth before I thought better of it.

"There was a time in my life when I would have jumped at the chance to get rid of that part of me. But it's been with me for so long now. And for the most part, I'm in control, not it."

"That wasn't an outright no."

"A part of me questions whether I'd still be half decent at this job if I didn't have the added animal-like reflexes that seem to bleed over, even when I'm human."

"Well, nothing says she's going to figure it out," I said weakly.

"Stay inside. Stay safe."

He gave me a pointed look that signaled we were done talking and I needed to go inside. I retreated to the foyer and watched through the tiny window beside the door as Rick stood sentinel on the front steps for a long minute. Finally, he left the porch and disappeared from view.

"I know what you're thinking," Tania called from the kitchen.

"So, you're a mind reader now too?" I teased.

"You can't let this go until you've solved it."

"I'm invested. Besides, it isn't like either of the suspects know I'm a witch or what I can do."

"That you know of."

"What's that supposed to mean?"

"You did not have Beau's invisibility when you and Maggie went to the scene to commune with nature and witness that man's death. Anyone could have seen you then. And for all you know that ghost haunting the carnival has been simply keeping an eye on you."

Why did I get the sense that was more Sam's sentiment than hers? "I'll admit, at first GhostCat freaked me out a bit. Especially when he could see Sam even when Sam was hiding in plain sight. But he hasn't been malicious or misleading. He warned us about Silvan's powers and that Tessa knows more than she's letting on. And he showed me the torn-up photograph in her trailer. I don't think he's working against us."

"Darcy, you need to respect Rick's orders. He is trying to protect us."

I walked into the kitchen to find her heating water for tea. Instinctively, I picked out two mugs from the cabinet by the sink and set them down on the counter beside the whistling kettle. "And I'm trying to protect him, too."

Tania busied herself by adding loose tea leaves to a pot. "You heard Rick, he can take care of himself. I know you have a deep devotion to the people you care about. It is an admirable quality, Darcy and one I hope you never lose. But if the last year has shown me anything, it's that we shouldn't take huge risks if they aren't necessary."

My brow furrowed. "Tania, this doesn't sound like you. Not even when you were going through everything after the kidnapping."

The kettle whistled and she plucked it from the stovetop, pouring the piping hot water into the teapot, letting it steep. "I know I have been your emotional rock through much of your time here. And you have given me a sense of adventure I honestly never thought I'd experience. But I do worry that your intense need to understand a mystery is going to hurt you some day or someone you love. And I may not be expressing only my own feelings on the matter. I am not the only one worried about your safety."

Who else? Maggie? She'd jumped into this case with me feet first. And Ginny had told me on more than one occasion to keep digging, because I had a penchant for solving mysteries.

"Rick? Vinnie?"

"They both value your input, even if they don't say it outright. But Rick does have a certain sense of defensiveness about you getting involved. And not just because of how you two first crossed paths. He still sees you as a civilian. He worries about you getting put in the middle of something you can't magic your way out of." She poured the freshly brewed tea into the mugs on the counter.

I wanted to argue with her and tell her that her feelings weren't valid. Only I knew that would have been selfish and a flat out lie. I took risks and they'd been growing bigger and bigger the longer I lived in Brookhaven. But they were worth it for me, because it meant protecting the people I loved, her included.

"I only keep getting involved, because it affects my people. All of you have given me a place to belong, and I am not going to give that up without a fight. And sometimes that means putting myself into spots that are a bit tight or dangerous. I can't say that I'll stop since I think we both know that isn't the way I am."

"I know you won't stop when the cause resonates with you. But you are not indestructible, and your magic is not infinite. It has limits and is fallible, like all magic. It's a product of nature. I just don't want you to find yourself unable to defend yourself. So please, just this once, stay put. Sit and have some tea with me, and let Rick and Vinnie do their jobs."

The last twenty-four hours had been a whirlwind of chaos and emotion. Maybe a strong cup of tea would be a nice respite. There wasn't anything else I could really do without tracking down Louis or Tessa. Besides, Rick wasn't without his own supernatural abilities.

"Maybe you're right," I said, accepting the mug Tania passed me.

We retreated to the living room, and I settled into the armchair that faced the front bay window. Sunlight dappled the carpet in front of me and I sunk into the soft cushions, enjoying the calm and quiet. I'd been running on adrenaline for so long, it was nice to just relax. I took a few sips of tea only to realize Tania had made Maggie's special chamomile blend. The kind I usually reserved for giving me a solid night's rest with a bit of healing boost.

"Are you trying to drug me?" I half-heartedly accused the woman sitting on the couch across from me.

"I'm trying to keep you out of trouble, Darcy. You are like family to me, and I don't want to lose you."

I managed to set the mug aside and wipe away the sleepiness just as my phone buzzed with an incoming text from Maggie and a call from Ginny. I swiped to answer the call first.

"You find something?" I asked through a poorly stifled yawn.

"More than you bargained for."

"Rick's got Tania and I on house arrest at the B&B, so you're going to need to come here."

"See you in five."

I turned my attention to Maggie's text.

> Think I've got some answers. Better to explain in person.

I responded.

> At the B&B. I've got things to share, too.

Tania eyed me warily. "Guess I'd better break out the coffee."

Here's hoping what they had figured out gave us a full picture of what really happened to Silvan.

13

True to her word, Ginny knocked on the front door five minutes later. I'd abandoned my tea, and the effects of the magically infused chamomile was already starting to fade. Ginny's cheeks were flushed as she stepped over the threshold and into the foyer. She carried a slender laptop under her arm.

"You didn't literally run over here, did you?" I prompted and ushered her into the kitchen where Tania had laid out some light refreshments along with a pot of freshly brewed coffee.

"I can't believe he locked you down," she said, ignoring my question.

"He's just worried about our safety. The details of the case are evolving in a dangerous direction,"

Tania explained just as the front door opened again and Maggie walked in, the black leather book tucked under her arm.

"He clearly hasn't seen Darcy in action enough times," Maggie retorted, joining us at the table.

"See, I tried to make that point and got reminded how I'm not indestructible." I gave my girlfriend a kiss. "But I do have the best healing hands in all of Brookhaven on my side."

"Now is not the time to get all flirty, ladies," Ginny quipped. "I found things and you're going to want to hear them."

"I've found something, too. But Ginny can go first." Maggie set the book on the table and pulled a mug towards her.

"So, Darcy asked me to look for anything with Silvan and Tessa together online. Well, they had a few promotional photos floating around that were like six or seven years old. He was standing under her while she was hanging by her fingertips from a trapeze."

"But she did the tight rope act when we saw her," I interrupted.

Ginny shrugged, unconcerned. "Doesn't matter. In a few of them, she was wearing a gold locket. It must have been pinned into her outfit. Even while she was hanging upside down, it wasn't falling over her face or anything."

We hadn't gotten a good look at what Louis had been trying to pawn Tyson. But maybe he'd be willing to share his security footage? "I wish we'd seen what Louis was trying to get Tyson to buy. I wonder if it was the same locket."

Tania let out a sigh. "I might be able to convince him to share his security footage."

"Brilliant."

"Darcy, that wedding photo, was she wearing it in that?" Maggie prompted.

"You said the photograph was torn up," Tania reminded me.

"Uh, I took a picture of the one Silvan had in his trailer." I pulled the image up on my phone and zoomed in on Tessa's face and torso. A slender gold chain with a locket hung just visible above the neckline of her wedding dress. I showed it to Ginny. She checked it before looking at something on her laptop. "Yeah, looks like the same one."

"So, maybe Tessa found out Louis had the locket, and she went to confront Silvan about it?" Maggie posed.

"It gets weirder," Ginny continued, clicking around her browser tabs to pull up some additional images. "After the big rebrand five years ago, the locket vanishes. At least from around Tessa's neck." She double clicked an image of Silvan standing in his ringmaster regalia, something glittering and gold stuck out of one of his jacket pockets. Like the way someone would wear an old pocket watch.

"My guess is he took it back after he changed his identity," Ginny offered.

"Tessa had to know him well if she married him. I can't imagine she wasn't aware of the type of magic he possessed," Tania said as she tapped out a message on her phone.

"Yeah, so maybe he needed something extra to keep her in line?" I suggested.

"It's definitely motive to want him dead if she somehow remembered what he'd done to her and the rest of the carnival crew. Maybe she happened upon him once he'd already been injured and that triggered her?" Maggie offered.

Ginny nodded wordlessly as she tabbed through a few other browser windows on her laptop. As we all sat around the kitchen table, I couldn't help but think about how exhausting it must have been for Silvan to keep the spell going constantly. He couldn't risk anyone remembering what he'd done. It wouldn't do to completely derail your entire operation. It would destroy their sense of family that's so integral to their way of life.

"I wish we knew how long after he had been wounded that he suffered his other injuries," I said mostly to myself.

"We saw the attack. It was fast. Remember, you sensed another presence before Rick showed up," Maggie said.

"Grass can't exactly tell time though," I answered.

"You want to know if this was coordinated," Tania posed. I nodded as she leaned over and showed Ginny something on her phone screen.

"Tell him to email it to me."

"What'd you find?" I probed.

"Tyson agreed to send over his security footage," Tania answered. "As for wondering if Tessa was working in tandem, I don't think you'll know that unless she confesses."

Which would mean leaving the B&B and putting myself right in Rick's crosshairs again. It wasn't a place I enjoyed being either, although it didn't terrify nearly as much as it had the first few times. Still, it would be better to stay on the cop's good side if at all possible.

Ginny's computer let out an audible 'ping' as she received Tyson's email. I scooted my chair around the edge of the table to have a more direct view of Ginny's screen. Maggie pressed in beside me as the blonde opened the video file Tyson had proffered. My heart hammered in my chest as we watched the exchange. It was clear video evidence of Louis trying to sell the locket. I couldn't hear anything being said—the pawn shop's surveillance clearly didn't come with audio—but the look of disgust on Tyson's face was clear enough to signal he wasn't interested in stolen goods.

"Can you pause it there?" I pointed at the screen just as Louis picked up the locket by the end of the chain.

Ginny tapped away at the keys, duplicating and minimizing browsers so she could pull up the image of the locket we'd seen on the promotional photos with Tessa and Ivan to compare it to the paused video image. I also held up the wedding photo I'd taken on my phone.

"It certainly looks like the same one to me," I said, giving the other women a hopeful look that they'd validate my impression.

"I think you're right. So, how did Louis get the locket?" Ginny murmured.

"I don't have an answer for that, but I do have some information you might find interesting about how Silvan was turning people into shifters," Maggie said, patting the leatherbound book.

Ginny's eyes lit up at Maggie's declaration. She turned in her chair, giving my girlfriend her full attention. "You figured out how he's doing it?"

"I think so." She opened the book to a middle page with tightly written cursive script. "It took me a bit to decipher the handwriting, but it is basically a recipe book for how to create a shifter." Her cheeks went sallow, and her lips pursed into a sour expression. "And it sounds horrible."

"I can handle whatever it is," Ginny insisted.

Maggie took a deep breath before she began explaining her findings. "Well, the bits of herbs and liquids we found were only part of the equation. According to Silvan's notes, they were used to both subdue the victim and provide healing once the spell was complete." She turned the pages where a few crude drawings were sketched on the right-hand page along with more of the cramped writing on the left-hand page. "The key to the transformation seems to be using the claws of an already supernatural creature."

"And he just happened to find a willing cougar to give up their claws for him?" I scoffed.

"I can't say exactly, but there were a few notes at

the back of the journal that suggested the type of creature they become is somewhat random. They typically retain the same broader genus. So, if you had the claw of a wolf, I suppose it would have more to do with dogs or other canine creatures."

"And he's got a cat," I groaned, feeling like a fool. It had been staring me in the face the whole time.

"What do you mean he's got a cat?" Ginny asked, her brow knitting together in confusion.

"You're telling me that creepy feline could be the reason our beloved chief is a big kitty cat when he gets cranky?" Sam trilled, appearing halfway through the kitchen counter abutting the dining room wall.

"Don't act like you haven't been making fun of my brother for his condition," Ginny snapped.

"Sam's right, though. I think GhostCat must be linked to Silvan's schemes."

"Well, it also might explain why you've been seeing the lynx's ghost," Maggie added softly. "It sounded like the supernatural subject's abilities passed primarily in death. And while I'm not an expert, I'm pretty sure one of the jars I found contained the claws of a large wild cat."

My chest tightened at the thought of GhostCat being bound to the carnival all because he'd been in the wrong place at the wrong time. It also made my stomach lurch at the thought that Silvan had done this to so many people. Marcus might not have been one of his victims, but there had to be plenty of people he'd harmed in this way. For all we knew, he'd learned it from whoever had in fact turned Marcus. That was likely one mystery we wouldn't solve.

One could argue that was motive in and of itself that extended beyond Tessa's spurned lover angle or Louis' anger about Marcus' abilities being overused in the show. But that was for the police and lawyers to sort out.

"Does it say anything about being able to reverse the spell?" Ginny made a grab for the book.

Maggie's face fell. "I'm sorry, Ginny. Believe me, I scoured every inch of his notes. But he never considered undoing it. And if I'm honest, playing with this sort of magic feels too dangerous ... a perversion of what magic is supposed to be. So even if it were possible to reverse it, I'm not sure I could do it."

Ginny let out a long exhale. "I understand. And Rick wouldn't want you to put yourself at risk like that on his account."

"For what it's worth, it sounds like he's at peace with this part of himself," I offered. "I'm not saying the trauma and the emotional wounds it left behind are fully healed, but he seems to appreciate the gifts it's given him—his enhanced senses, the way he fights to protect the town. So, it's not all bad."

"I wish we knew what prompted Ivan to fake his own death and reinvent himself as Silvan," Maggie said, changing the topic of discussion.

"I might have figured that part out, too," Ginny said, pulling up another web page featuring a court hearing from New Hampshire. She read aloud from the case summary.

"On March 2, the defendant, Ivan Gregor was charged with criminally negligent homicide in the death of performer Marcelina Shaw. Shaw had worked for Gregor's traveling carnival as an acrobatic performer when she died under suspicious circumstances while alone with Gregor, according to witness reports."

"How much do you want to bet he tried to turn her into a shifter and something went wrong?" I said darkly.

"Wait, there's more in the record. It looks like a warrant was issued for his arrest for contempt of court, because he refused to show up to any of the proceedings. I found the article you mentioned about his death by fire. It fits the timeline of the case history. After his death, the case was closed and dropped."

"That seems strange," Tania said and everyone's attention fell on her. "Even if he died, surely his estate had access to the funds tied up in the carnival. And he presumably left behind a spouse."

"But none of the Carnival staff even remembered he was the same person as the man who showed up pretending to be Ivan's cousin, I wouldn't put it past him to also manipulate the court personnel, too," I answered. "I hate to speak ill of the dead, but part of me really isn't that broken up that a bad man's dead for real this time. At least now he can't hurt anyone else."

"So, we know that he likely faked his death to get out of the court battle," Ginny noted, her voice tinged with disgust. "Well, that would give Tessa plenty of reason to want to off him for real if she realized who he truly was."

"That still doesn't explain who actually mauled him before she showed up. No one else admitted to being a shifter on the staff except for Marcus."

"We know Louis wasn't happy about how often Marcus was being made to transform. Maybe he confronted Silvan about it after their act went on and things got physical? Or Marcus was so upset about his husband taking things too far he snapped?" Maggie suggested. "Just because Vinnie didn't find any evidence on him doesn't mean he couldn't have done it, right?"

"Possible, but I think we need to find a way to draw them all out. Get them to confess what they've done."

"What are you thinking?" Sam floated closer, his dark red glittery eye makeup somehow catching the sunlight coming in through the window.

"There had to be a reason Louis was trying to pawn Silvan's locket. He came into possession of it somehow. Also, he knows that Tania and I saw him with Tyson. What if I offered to buy it off him?"

"That takes care of him, but what about Tessa?" Ginny pressed.

Beside me, Maggie's phone rang with an incoming call from the clinic. She excused herself and answered the phone. Her cheeks drained of color a moment later. "You did the right thing calling me. I'll be right there."

She ended the call and turned back to face us. "Finding Tessa isn't going to be a problem. She just showed up at the clinic with some serious cuts. My staff isn't equipped to handle that level of trauma on their own."

"You can't go alone," I said, standing as I spoke. "We could swing by High Time, pick up some edibles. Maybe she'll be open to using them for pain management. And if we're lucky, it will loosen her lips."

Tania stood to my left. "I don't like the idea of leading a man on. And I don't approve of any of us going into this without Rick and Vinnie as back-up. Darcy, I can't stop you from going to the clinic with Maggie, but I am going to tell them what you're planning."

"Why don't I go by and see if I can get Louis to talk to me? I'd know if he was lying," Ginny offered. "And the longer I keep him talking, the more chance Rick has to come along and overhear any potential confession."

It wasn't our best plan of attack ever, but it would have to do. Time to divide and, with any luck, conquer.

14

My heart pounded in my chest as Maggie and I walked up to the front entrance of High Time. The employee entrance was unlocked, but it felt a little odd going that way. Besides, I was actually looking to buy edibles, not just pluck a few leaves from one of the growing plants. Sage gave us both a quizzical look when I stepped up to the counter.

"Not your usual spot and you're not working till tomorrow," she noted, hooking her thumb back over her shoulder to the door leading to the grow room.

"Yeah, I know. I, uh, was actually looking to make a purchase." My cheeks warmed at my own words.

"Oh, totally. After everything that happened

yesterday, I'm not surprised you need a little something to calm your nerves."

"Everything that happened?" I leaned on the
edge of the counter.

"You know small town, it talks, Darcy. Word got
out pretty quickly you were part of the group that
found the dead ringmaster at the carnival." She
shuddered with her whole body. "I couldn't
imagine."

Maggie glanced at her phone and a text from her
co-worker flashed on the screen. "Not to rush you,
but we actually have somewhere we need to be
pretty soon."

"Oh, right. What were you thinking?"

"Just some of the lower dose gummies." I passed
over my ID and a twenty dollar bill. "Keep the
change."

Sage smiled at me and stuck the bill in the till.
"Give me two minutes."

I watched my boss disappear from view and let
out a breath I hadn't realized I'd been holding. "This
feels so strange," I noted, but Maggie was still
focused intently on her phone. "Everything okay?"

"Yeah, the nurse is just having a hard time
keeping her there."

"Thank you," I said and reached over to pull her

into a hug. "For sticking with me through all this craziness."

"It's our craziness, Darcy. We're in it together, no matter what."

Just then, Sage returned with a small brown bag and passed it over the counter. "One should take the edge off. Don't take more than two at a time."

"Yes, ma'am," I promised and snatched up the bag.

My heart stopped metaphorically ricocheting off my ribs as we left High Time. For some reason approaching a potential killer was less terrifying than buying product I'd helped to craft from my boss. My mind raced, trying to put a picture together of how badly Tessa was injured. The specks of blood I'd noticed in her trailer surely wouldn't be enough to seek medical care. But there was another possibility. A fight could have ensued if she'd tried to take the locket back from Marcus and Louis.

"We need to have a game plan before we get in there," Maggie said and nudged my arm to get my attention.

"Right. Well, we need to see how badly she's injured first. Hopefully, we can convince her to take some of the gummies as a way to relax and soothe the pain. Maybe then we can get her talking. See if she will take us back to the carnival and show us whatever evidence she might have kept linking her to the crime."

"It's too bad that you didn't find out more information about those impressions on Silvan's neck."

The information had been shared so quickly and then Rick had insisted that Tania and I leave. There wasn't time to get a good look at the photos of Silvan's body. Not that I'd really wanted to commit them to memory. "There weren't any other actual footprints in the area, remember? My guess if Tessa was there, maybe she wasn't even wearing shoes?"

"What makes you think that?"

"Just a feeling. Things happened so quickly after the show started. She didn't have any shoes on during her act. I'd imagine that she wasn't wearing shoes when she found him. Especially if Silvan's death was premeditated in any way. Everyone knows about shoe impressions from movies and television. It's not a leap to assume she would have gone to confront him in her costume straight from the big top."

We reached the clinic, and Maggie ushered me around back. I'd never approached the building from this direction, and I spotted a small loading dock for supply trucks. She led me to a locked rear entrance with a keypad. I averted my gaze as she entered the code before she pulled the heavy door open, and I followed her inside. Not surprisingly, it led from the very back of the clinic via a small, cramped hall behind the main examination room.

It wasn't hard to gauge where Tessa was waiting. A loud clattering came from the room directly in front of us, followed by a young man's voice. "Miss, I promise, the clinician who can stitch you up is on their way. You just need to wait a few more minutes."

"I knew this was a mistake," Tessa shouted in exasperation.

Maggie took off her jacket, donned a white coat, and picked up a suture kit with lots of gauze. Next, she rounded the corner and stepped into view of the exam room. Mercifully, no other customers were around to witness the commotion.

"Hi there, I'm Maggie. I'm going to be helping you," she announced, holding up the medical supplies.

I stayed back, not wanting to crowd the space. The young man cleared his throat. "... Okay, I'll leave you to it." As he passed Maggie he added in a whisper, "Sorry about all the blood."

He gave me a semi-curious glance as he walked past before hurrying off to stock shelves nearby. My heartbeat picked up again as his words sunk in. I swallowed down the lump of fear in my throat and took a few steps closer and peered inside. Tessa had several large gashes bleeding on her arms and legs, and a blood soaked ripped shirt. They looked suspiciously like claw marks.

"Hi," I said in as neutral a tone as I could muster. I focused on Tessa's unblemished face. If I just kept looking her in the eye, I wouldn't have to think about the wounds and blood.

"You again?" Tessa sounded irritated.

"I was with Maggie when she got the call that you needed some help. You'd been so helpful at the carnival, I came along to offer you some support. Things couldn't have been easy the past day with so much upheaval in all of your lives. And now, it looks like you've been attacked."

"Hazard of working with wild animals," Tessa answered, not looking away.

"You said Marcus wouldn't ever hurt anyone. That he liked being the way he was. Why would he attack you?" After a beat I added, "Unless there's someone else like him in your company?"

She finally looked away and let out a loud hiss as Maggie cleaned the wound on her left forearm.

"You're lucky this isn't deeper. You could have been in a lot of trouble otherwise."

"Just fix it up. Please."

I held out the small brown bag. "I work at the local dispensary and have some of the low-grade gummies if you're interested?"

"Why the hell not?" she said and made a grabbing motion. "But only if you do one, too."

The bottom dropped out of my stomach. I'd never been high, and I wasn't about to start now. Not when I was trying to ensnare a killer. Maggie looked at me and mouthed, 'Palm it.' I opened the bag and pulled out two of the greenish round gummies, passing one to Tessa. She watched me carefully as I opened my mouth and mimed tossing it back. I kept it securely between my fingers. I mimed chewing and swallowing. Satisfied, she took her own gummy, still wincing as Maggie continued to clean and dress each of her wounds.

I turned my back long enough to return the gummy to the bag before I addressed Tessa. "So, now that Silvan is dead, what will happen to the carnival?"

"Why are you so interested?"

"Just making conversation, that's all. I honestly don't know much about how traveling carnivals operate. It seems like a lot of moving pieces and responsibility."

"I've managed it before." The way she said it came out as almost a surprise declaration as if the words slipped out before she had thought them through. I knew the strength of the gummies, there was no way this was the result of her being high. The marijuana might be magically grown, but it didn't kick in that fast.

"Before Silvan showed up after Ivan's death, someone must have had to keep things going. I'm guessing that was you."

She let out a disgusted snort. "You really think he and Ivan were just relatives who looked alike?"

"I don't know, but I have a feeling you've got a strong opinion on the matter."

"That man was a cheat. You know what, I only put on a sad face for everyone because they're all so gullible and still believe the lies he fed us."

"But you know differently?" Maggie joined the conversation.

"My eyes are open, I'm not asleep like the rest of them. I'm glad he's dead for real this time. I'm done letting him take everything from me."

I hadn't anticipated her being quite so forthcoming. "So, you two had history?"

"Oh, you could say that." After a moment she asked Maggie, "Am I going to have scars?"

I could feel the warmth coming off Maggie's hands as she stepped back from the other woman. "You aren't the only ones who know about the supernatural. I've infused these wraps and sutures with a bit of extra healing. If they do scar, it should be hardly noticeable."

"Great. Well, thanks for the help and for the relaxer too. I need to get back to everyone."

"You shouldn't walk alone since you lost a lot of blood. I want to make sure you have somewhere you can rest and elevate everything," Maggie said hurriedly.

"Fine. I guess an escort couldn't hurt. At least you'd be my alibi if the cops came sniffing around again."

"Why would they come looking for you?" I pressed, praying the gummy would kick in soon.

"Because they've been digging around all day. They're bound to figure out our connection."

"That you were married to Ivan?" I blurted. I regretted the admission instantly. I had no reason to have that information unless I, too, had been digging.

"News spreads fast in small towns, doesn't it?"

"I overheard the police mentioning they found a record you two were married. Sometimes my landlady takes them special food. She's an excellent cook," I rambled, trying to cover my tracks.

"Technically, we were still married since he was alive and masquerading as someone else right under my nose. I'm not proud I fell for it. I should have been stronger, but he used my own grief against me. Against us all."

Maggie disappeared momentarily, returning with a clean shirt that she offered to Tessa. "So, you don't have to walk around covered in blood."

Tessa stripped off the ruined top and accepted the clean shirt. It was baggy over her thin frame. Apparently her time as a performer had curbed her modesty. Maggie gave me a look and shooing motion. "Come on, I'll walk you back."

I practically shoved Tessa out of the examination room, leaving Maggie to carefully pick up the shirt and place it into a plastic bag. A moment later I realized she was trying to preserve evidence. Maybe the attacker had left DNA behind? "I don't mean to pry, but you didn't seem to remember any of this the first time we talked before the carnival opened the other day."

"I guess you could say his death allowed everything to open up."

Part of me wanted to believe her, but it didn't fit the theory that she was involved with his demise. We fell silent as we hurried along Main Street, past Ginny's cafe and the police station. Both buildings had their lights on, but looked empty as we passed. My mouth went dry for a minute as I wondered if Ginny had any luck with Louis and Marcus.

"You know, if you wanted to press charges against whoever attacked you, I know the police here would believe you."

"Carnival people avoid the cops whenever possible. They only bring trouble."

"I've had my fair share of run-ins where I wished I hadn't gotten mixed up with the law," I confessed. "But generally, they're just trying to find the truth. Wouldn't you want that to come to light, especially if Silvan and Ivan were the same person?"

We reached the edge of the Tyson's property, and she turned to face me. "I don't know what you think you're going to get out of this conversation, but we've made it back to the carnival grounds. I'm fine. Your doctor friend doesn't need to check up on me either."

I spotted Rick approaching along the backside of

the stalls on the main thoroughfare. "Except the police are here and they think you had something to do with Silvan's death."

"Me?"

"I'll explain everything, but we need somewhere to go where they aren't going to find us."

My phone buzzed in my pocket and a text from Ginny popped up. Tessa stood beside me, turning this way and that, trying to spot the police I'd just mentioned. It gave me enough time to open Ginny's message and see that she wanted me to meet her in the big top with Tessa.

"How about the big top? I'm sure they've already looked in there for you."

Tessa nodded and she ducked her head as we hurried in the opposite direction of Rick. I met the lawman's gaze, and he gave me a scowl, but didn't attempt to approach us. He was going to let this play out, but he'd be there in an instant if things went wrong. At least I knew he had my back. Now I just hoped I could finally get Tessa to confess her involvement in Silvan's death. Good thing I had a witch who could extract the truth waiting for us.

We slipped through the front flap of the tent, and I quickly surveyed the surroundings. The grass had been trampled from the audience coming through the day before, but I could feel the life still in it. If needed, I would call on my magic to restrain Tessa. I sensed that we weren't alone.

"I'm listening," Tessa prompted, looking over my right shoulder.

Before I could speak, she let out an anguished moan and made a lunge for something I couldn't see. I pivoted on the spot in time to see her trying to make it to Ginny who held the locket aloft. Louis stood across from her, his hands no longer human, but feline, with very sharp, bloody claws.

"That's mine!" Tessa howled and made another grab for the locket. Ginny wasn't fast enough to get out of the woman's way and they both fell to the ground.

15

*E*verything moved in half time as I stood immobile, watching as Tessa dug at the locket in Ginny's grip. The blonde struggled beneath the other woman's weight. She wasn't strong enough to keep the object from its original owner. Tessa snatched it. Without touching the ground, she pushed herself up and hovered, much like Sam was prone to do, a good six inches off the ground.

Ginny scrambled to her feet and placed distance between herself and Tessa. Louis, for his part, stood there eyeing all of us with an animalistic hunger. Apparently, he wasn't just the human part of the act. The fur that sprouted on the backs of his hands looked pale, almost like a lion. Had he willingly given himself to Silvan in an effort to give his husband a reprieve?

"Louis attacked you," I called, trying to regain Tessa's attention.

"He had something that belonged to me, and I wanted it back. He had no right to take it."

"He took everything from me. Silvan owed me." Louis' voice came out in a low growl.

"By all accounts, he brought you Marcus," I said, turning my focus on him. "You two met at a show. That's what he told me, anyway. And he was already a shifter. So, he could fill a void. And it meant he got to be with you, because he loves you."

"That bastard took advantage of Marcus. Marcus was always a people pleaser. He didn't know when to say no. So, I had to do it for him. Otherwise, they would have worked him to death."

"Is that how you got him to give you an alibi?" Ginny prompted. "He would never betray you and lied about where you were to the police?"

"No, he told the truth. We went back to the trailer after our act. We had a drink, fooled around, and he fell asleep."

"You say you love him, but we both know you drugged him," Tessa accused, hovering in mid-air. Even though she was still close to the ground, she looked ready to launch herself into the air in a graceful arc. The bandages didn't distract from the graceful way her body moved.

"I knew if he followed me, he'd try to stop me. I just gave him a little sedative. Not enough to mess with his memory or hurt him," Louis argued. His hands flexed and his claws appeared to extend more.

Ginny looked at me and mouthed 'Do something.' In that moment I regretted that her power was more passive than mine. As inconspicuously as I could, I reached out my hands and felt for the magic around me that still lived in the grass beneath my feet. Power snapped to attention, much like it had when I'd given Rick the lifeline to keep him grounded the night of the murder. The grass braided together around my feet, elongating itself to make a rope so that I could loop around either one of the dangers. I just had to decide which of them was in need of restraint more.

"So, you followed Silvan after Marcus was out of the way and just decided to kill him?" I asked, looking at Louis.

He jutted his chin towards the locket Tessa clutched to her bandaged torso. "I stole that from him. Some part of me knew it meant something to him. I figured he'd want it back. He always wore it, even when he wasn't in full costume. I'm not ashamed to admit I did a bit of pickpocketing in my youth. It wasn't hard to take it off him."

"Did you know it would have an effect on anyone else?" Ginny seemed to be putting the pieces together, too.

"What are you talking about?"

"Me, you great oaf," Tessa snapped. "You took this from him and something like a barrier inside my head disappeared. I was remembering things I didn't know I'd forgotten. Things that exposed Silvan for the fraud he was."

"I had no idea it did anything to you. I didn't care about anyone but Marcus."

Louis began to pace, the skin on his upper arms rippling as fur sprouted from every pore. Any time now I expected him to drop to all fours and sprout a thick mane. But he was more in control of the change than I'd ever seen someone with shifting ability.

"Once you had the locket, how'd you lure him out?" Ginny questioned.

Louis' head snapped to look at the blonde woman. "I made a show of having it tucked into my costume during our act. I knew he would still be in the tent, and he'd see it. He followed us back to our trailer."

"But Marcus doesn't remember seeing the ringmaster," I noted. The braided length of grass around my feet grew more vibrant as I fed it more power, strengthening the bonds within it.

"He waited until I left our trailer, and I told him I'd give it back, but we needed to talk somewhere private. He suggested by his trailer since no one ever goes back there during a show. He demanded the locket back, but I refused to give it up without his word that he'd stop forcing Marcus to change every night."

"I guess I should thank you for putting an end to my own misery," Tessa interrupted. "You took him out."

Louis shook his head. "I told him I'd meet him there. He wasn't expecting me to change, but I was prepared. I just wanted to scare him into doing what I wanted, I didn't mean to hurt him like that."

"Except you didn't kill him," I said. "At least you weren't the only cause. The police found evidence someone crushed his windpipe. He was still alive when you left him."

"They can't know that," Tessa blurted, rising higher into the air, seemingly out of our reach.

In the rafters I spotted GhostCat slinking along the trapeze platform, dancing along agilely as his thick tail swished. I spotted movement at the far end of the tent. Marcus appeared and I spotted Rick behind him. At least the lawman would be here for the rest of the confession.

"I saw the crime scene photos," I lied. "He had some sort of impression on his neck and there was bruising."

"You're just making that up," she screeched.

"I can understand why both of you would want to hurt him, but what I can't put my finger on is why you both chose that moment? Why Brookhaven? Was it just because this town has a supernatural reputation, and you figured they wouldn't blink at a man being mauled by a supposed wild animal?"

"Well, this place had a ready-made suspect," Louis answered. Fur sprouted along his bare chest now. If I didn't do something soon, I'd be trapped in here with a very angry and large cat who'd already nearly killed someone.

"You knew about Chief Hayes."

"Who do you think lured him? Silvan didn't do anything without roping someone in. So, he could have something to hold over your head. That way you didn't ever think about leaving."

"You forced Rick to undergo the spell to change him? He was a stranger, an innocent."

"But he's what Silvan wanted. I didn't question it back then."

Tessa made a sweeping gesture at Louis, and said, "No way he would have done this to you."

"He's not the only one who could work the spell. I saw him do it enough times and knew all the steps. And I was willing. I knew what it took."

"So, you were going to take on the role, to give Marcus a rest?" I posed.

Louis scoffed, "No. I knew I needed extra strength to take Silvan on. He'd kept everyone under his thumb for long enough."

He looked up at Tessa. "But you weren't supposed to see anything. And should have just left it alone."

"He took everything from me—my choice, my life. You stealing the locket broke it all open and I knew I had to confront him. Finding him wasn't hard. I saw him go after you, so I just waited."

"You used your ability to keep from leaving footprints behind," I said. "And you didn't wear shoes, because you knew they'd leave impressions. I admit, that was pretty clever."

"He was just lying there bleeding all over the

grass. He looked so scared and begged me for help. At least he tried to anyway. For a minute, I thought about actually helping him. But that was just the spell he'd cast over us still clinging to my mind. Once I remembered everything he'd done to me, I was over it. So, I put him out of his misery. In the end, I showed him more mercy than he ever gave the rest of us."

"I can't believe you'd do any of this!" Marcus shouted, racing to the center of the tent. He looked horrified at the state of his husband, displaying every inch of himself as the caricature of a half man, half beast. "I told you I was okay with what we were doing. It was my decision, not yours." Tears sparkled in his eyes. "I never wanted this for you."

"I did it to protect you," Louis protested.

He looked like he wanted to revert back to his human form. Yet the change seemed to only come over him more, the fabric of his pants ripping as his legs thickened and he fell to all fours. His face elongated, fur rippling over his skin as his eyes went yellow. He shook out his thick dark mane and made a lunge for Tessa, a deep growl reverberating in his chest.

Time to act.

I waved my hands and the rope I'd magically

woven flew into the air, wrapping around his torso like a lasso. I tried to yank it back, but the slender fibers of the braid snapped under the beast's weight. I fell backwards, slamming my right arm into the nearest bench. Pain lanced up my arm and I gritted my teeth to keep from letting out a scream. Louis as a lion had managed to snare Tessa's ankles and hauled her back to the ground.

I'd orchestrated this whole scenario, and there wasn't any chance I would let it end with more bloodshed. Planting my hands firmly on the ground with my palms pressed into the dirt, I pictured the grass growing up thick all around Tessa's body, becoming a shield. I envisioned thick vines and roses, their thorns sharp and defensive popping around every place Louis tried to reach. I'd managed to transform normal grass into other plants at my coming out display on Halloween and it seemed the skill remained.

Tessa struggled beneath the barrier I'd created, trying to escape but with no luck. Louis' paws caught some of the thorns and he let out a dismayed grunt as he staggered back. Marcus moved to stand in front of the lion.

"I know you can hear me, Louis. I need you to stop now. You have to stop."

"He's not going to listen," Ginny called, trying to grab the other man by the arm and pull him out of the way.

"Why'd you burn the photo?" I yelled at Tessa. "Just letting your anger out?"

"I found it in his trailer, at the bottom of a drawer after he'd thrown me away. He deserved it all." She thrashed against the grass still growing around her. "Let me out of here!"

Louis was coming around for another pounce. My magic was enough to subdue Tessa, but I wasn't a match for the man who'd willingly underwent dark magic in the name of love. In the space between one breath and the next, Louis made another pass at Tessa. But this time, something hit the lion from the side, knocking him off kilter. I watched Rick as he somehow pinned the supernatural creature to the ground with his bare arms. When he looked at me, his eyes were totally amber and where his fingernails should have been, dark claws had sprouted, digging just deep enough into Louis' fur to keep him immobile.

"I thought I told you to leave this to the professionals!" he snapped at me.

"Maybe we can argue about this when you're not wrestling a bloody lion?" I called.

Rick gave a grunt of agreement and his claws sunk a little deeper. Louis let out a pained yowl and slowly, the massive beast began to shrink, and the fur slipped back beneath the skin. Rick soon straddled a naked man. He pulled out a pair of handcuffs and secured them around Louis' wrists.

"Let her up when Vinnie gets here. We'll be taking them both into custody."

Ginny moved out of her brother's way as he led Louis from the tent. Marcus sat on the ground, looking forlorn and heartbroken. I couldn't blame him for being emotional. His whole world had turned upside down in an instant.

"I can't blame you for being furious at what Silvan ... I mean Ivan did to you all. But that doesn't justify killing him. You could have just left," I told Tessa as the front flap of the tent moved and Vinnie appeared, handcuffs at the ready.

"You don't just leave him. He owned all of us in one way or another. Death was the only way."

Slowly, I let the magic recede when I saw Vinnie. The thorns and roses vanished, and the grass slid off her body like a wave, disappearing back into the ground beneath her. I half expected her to make a run for it as Vinnie approached, but she remained where she lay. He eased her to her feet and secured her hands behind her back.

Moments later, Ginny and I stood alone in the tent. She wrapped her arms around her torso. "Thank you for helping Rick solve this one. Even though we couldn't give him what I really wanted, I think he's at peace now."

"What do you mean?"

"The day he was turned, I'd begged him to go with me to the carnival. If I hadn't ... he wouldn't have ended up how he did."

"You can't blame yourself for other people's actions. And I'm sure Rick doesn't blame you either. He wouldn't want you to carry that guilt."

"Sometimes forgiving yourself is harder than forgiving the people who caused the wounds in the first place."

I pulled her into a hug and held her tight. "For someone who can pull the truth out of anyone, I'd think you'd be better at telling it to yourself."

"It's never worked on me. I'm the only person who can lie to my face."

" Forgive yourself, because you helped give your brother the answers he needed as much as any of us."

The morning was quiet—more so than it had been since the carnival came to town—and I let out a sigh of relief as I opened my eyes. My bedroom at the B&B greeted me and I snuggled deeper under my blankets. The adrenaline of the last few days in the wake of the murder investigation had worn off, and I'd finally been able to sleep soundly. It didn't hurt that we'd managed to clear Rick and give him closure on the trauma in his past.

My phone buzzed on the side table with an incoming text. I lazily grabbed for it, succeeding in sending it tumbling to the floor. Groaning, I leaned down to retrieve it to find a message from Ginny of all people.

Meet at the cafe in an hour.

Well, that seemed like a strange request. Sure, we'd become friends over the last few months, but she had never invited me for breakfast. Still, I couldn't refuse her request. So, I dragged myself out of bed and stumbled into the bathroom, letting the shower's warm water wash away the early morning brain fog.

When I stepped off the bottom step of the stairs into the front hall Sam greeted me. He sported a vibrant blue blazer and sequined trousers. His eye makeup matched the blazer, and he had tiny rhinestones trailing down his cheeks like tears. "You've been summoned," he chirped.

"Come again?"

"I was on my way back from the waterfront and I saw Ginny sending off a bunch of texts. She had your number in there too."

I held my phone up. "Yeah, it's why I'm out of bed on a Sunday before eight o'clock," I explained.

Sam pouted at me. "Fine, sap all the joy out of my existence, why don't you?"

"Oh, come on, Sam. Don't pout. You aren't really that mad I saw the text already. What's bothering you?"

"I guess I'm just anxious for all the carnival drama to be over. I don't like being seen when I don't want the attention."

I could understand how it could be unnerving for his ghostly invisibility to stop working, but it had only been GhostCat. The unusual spectral feline had actually proved useful in uncovering the truth about Silvan's murder. "He wasn't trying to upset you."

Sam rolled his eyes. "He's a cat. It's practically in their DNA."

"Well, they'll be out of town in a week. You can survive that long."

He crossed his arms over his chest. "I like being the only ghost in town, thanks. I just want things back to the status quo."

If I could have given him a sympathetic pat on the shoulder, I would have. As it was, I would be late for Ginny's impromptu summoning. "You'll be fine," I called as I donned a jacket and left the B&B behind.

The morning air was brisk as I made my way to Main Street. The lights inside Ginny's cafe were on when I arrived, although the sign on the front door still said closed. A moment later, the proprietor appeared and flipped the lock, letting me inside. The center counter was laid out with baked goods and carafes of coffee and tea.

"I hope that's not all for me," I joked as Ginny pulled the door shut again leaving it unlocked.

"You aren't the only one coming," she replied, and tapped her index finger against her chin. "But maybe I did go a little overboard with the muffins and the croissants."

Before I could ask who else had been summoned, the door behind me opened and Maggie walked in. I gave my girlfriend a broad grin and reached out to pull her into an embrace. "Morning." I planted a kiss on her lips.

"Morning," she replied and returned the gesture. "Any idea what's going on?" We moved off to the side and slid into a booth to give Ginny some space to fret over the trays of food.

"Not really. But I won't say no to food and good company," I answered.

"How are you holding up after everything?" She fixed me with a concerned expression.

"I'm fine. I promise." I was getting used to big displays of magic and found they took less out of me these days. And a bit of Maggie's healing magic had set my arm to right in no time. I was just glad that she'd been there for me in the aftermath.

In short order, Vinnie and Rick joined us and Ginny hastily locked the door again. The gesture made my stomach do a nervous flip as she turned to face us.

"I just wanted to say thank you to everyone for what you did for Rick." She made eye contact with me. "I know we all haven't had the easiest of relationships, but you really came through for our family again Darcy."

"I did what anyone would have done. Rick is a good man." I turned to look her brother in the face. The glint of amber in his gaze was present, but it no longer frightened me or made me uneasy. "He deserved to know the truth. I'm just glad we were able to help put this all to bed."

"I spent a lot of my life ashamed of something I had no control over. You allowed me to regain some of that power I thought I'd lost." His voice cracked at the end, and I noticed his hands ball into fists as he tried to keep his emotions in check.

As I looked out the front window, I spotted Marcus walking up the street, dressed in civilian clothes. His hands were shoved into his pockets, and he stopped when he spotted us in the cafe. I could see a look of sadness etched into his features. I couldn't blame him for feeling grief over the loss of the man he loved. In a way, I could understand what drove Louis to confront Silvan. The man had exploited everyone in the carnival all for his own profit. That would drive almost anyone to fight back. And knowing Tessa's history with Silvan's alter ego explained the pain she'd felt at his betrayal. It didn't justify either of their actions, but I could still sympathize with them.

Turning back to the spread Ginny had prepared, I gestured to the front door. "You said yourself you made too much. Maybe we ought to consider sharing?"

Ginny's gaze flitted to the door. Marcus stood outside, clearly debating if he wanted to interact with our group. After a moment of hesitation, Ginny crossed the short distance and flipped the lock, pulling the door inward. "Come in please."

Marcus hesitated on the threshold before stepping inside and allowing Ginny to shut the door once more, locking it. He kept his gaze fixed on a spot on the floor just in front of his shoes. Maggie nudged Rick in the arm and pointed toward the other man.

Vinnie cleared his throat, stepping forward. "I know it doesn't make it any easier, but I am sorry about how things shook out."

Marcus looked up. "Not your fault, deputy. You didn't make Louis do anything. He made his choices and now we both have to live with them." He turned to Rick. "I am sorry for everything you went through all those years ago. If any of us had realized ... well, maybe we could have done something different."

"It took me a long time to come to terms with what happened. And during that time, I spent a lot of it, thinking about what might have been. But you can't change the past and there's no sense in dwelling on it now. We all need to move forward."

Not wanting the food to be forgotten, I stepped around Rick and picked up a plate, loading it with a blueberry muffin and some fresh berries. The others took it as their cue to follow suit and before long, we'd pushed two smaller tables together on the far right side of the cafe.

"So, what will happen to the carnival now that Silvan and Tessa are gone?" I wrapped my hands around one of Ginny's signature oversized mugs as I addressed Marcus.

"I'm not sure. I've talked to the other performers. Some of them want to stay together. Our group is the only family some of them has ever had. But there's so much darkness around the show ... I wouldn't mind stepping out of the spotlight."

"Are you going to stay with him?" Maggie's question carried no hint of judgement as she looked at the man.

"I don't condone what he did, and I can't stop feeling guilty since I was the reason behind what he did. But he's my husband and I love him. He's already going to be so isolated. I can't abandon him."

"Family's important," Ginny agreed. "Sometimes it's all we have." She cast a knowing look in Rick's direction.

"If the carnival does split up, what's going to happen to GhostCat?" The spectral feline had been something of an oddity, even in Brookhaven, and I couldn't help but wonder what might befall the creature now.

Marcus perked up at the mention of the ghostly cat. "Oh, he goes where I go. So, he'll be just fine. It will be nice to have a familiar face around. And I know he doesn't look like it, but he can be quite the amusing companion when I'm in my other form."

I narrowly avoided spitting my coffee across the table as I pictured Marcus in his tiger form playing like a kitten with GhostCat. The rest of my companions must have had similar mental images, because Vinnie and Maggie burst out laughing. Even Rick gave a soft chuckle.

"Are you sure he wasn't used in your transformation?" I probed.

"Honestly, anything's possible. All I know is we've got an affinity and I don't want to lose that." After a beat, Marcus' smile faded. "I know we were supposed to stay through the end of the week, but we can pack up and go sooner if you want us out of your town."

Rick waved a hand. "It's no secret I dislike your operation, but it wasn't so much the carnival people as it was your former management. And like you said, you need to sort out what everyone's doing next. Here's as good a place as any to hash out those details. Besides, this town has always been a safe harbor for the supernatural. Wouldn't be very neighborly of us if we just kicked you out? If the town council was right, the carnival is bringing in a nice revenue boost for the town and we could use that these days."

Relief washed over Marcus' face, and he wiped at the corners of his eyes. "Thank you."

Silence fell over the cafe as everyone turned their attention to finishing their breakfast. Out of the corner of my eye, I spotted some of Ginny's Sunday regulars congregating on the sidewalk outside. Some even pointed to the sign on the door and the obvious locked front door. Ginny let out a long sigh. "Well, I better let them in."

The counter still boasted half of its baked goods and at least one carafe of coffee as the regulars streamed inside, sitting in their usual haunts.

"Bit of a change today," Ginny announced. "We've got some free baked goods for anyone who'd like them."

A brief murmur went up from the patrons before they descended on the free goods. I stared at my empty plate and mug. On impulse, I stood and carried them towards the back of the cafe. I might not work here, but I felt bad leaving Ginny to do all the cleanup. She snatched the dishes from my hands before I'd made it past the end of the counter.

"Customers don't do the dishes." The way her lips twitched as she spoke, I got the sense she'd almost said something else, possibly friends.

"Habit," I said.

"Besides, you already have a job, and I don't think Sage would be happy having to share her miracle worker."

Even though everyone in town knew about my magical abilities, I still felt self-conscious when they brought up the fact, I was using my abilities to help boost High Time's bottom line. "It was doing just fine before me," I mumbled.

"Take the compliment Darcy," Ginny chided. "Anyway, thanks for coming," she said again as she set the dirty dishes in a bin she'd retrieved from behind the counter.

"I'm just happy it all worked out."

She arched a honey-colored brow at me and jutted out her chin. "Looks like you've got someone waiting for your attention."

I pivoted to see Maggie standing by the tables we'd pushed together. She held out her hand and I took it in mine, letting her lead me from the cafe. I didn't speak until we were halfway to the edge of town.

"What are you doing?" I pulled my hand free and stopped walking.

"I know you didn't exactly have the best time at the carnival, but I thought maybe now all the death is behind us, we could try again ... Maybe go for one more ride on the Ferris Wheel?"

"At nine in the morning?"

She grinned at me. "Won't be a line."

I couldn't shake the butterflies in my stomach as she hurried along and stepped through the open gates. A few of the carnival staff eyed us warily as we walked through the grounds to the large wheel rising high into the sky. The operator was already standing by and the motors revved as we approached. Why did I get the sense he knew we'd be coming? He secured the lap bar across our legs and the ride began to send us skyward, groaning and lurching as it had done on our first ride.

When we reached the top, the ride halted, and I could take in the scene below. The workers looked like miniature figurines darting about their day. I turned as best I could to Maggie and gave her a nervous smile.

"Why do I get the sense there's something else going on here?"

Maggie laughed. "I promise, nothing else is going on. I just wanted to enjoy the view from up here with the woman I love. Without all the chaos going on down there. Our lives are so full of magic and wonder, but sometimes it's nice to just take a breath and appreciate the quiet moments, too."

I leaned against her shoulder and wound my fingers with hers, holding them tight. I closed my eyes and let the sensation of her sitting beside me fill my other senses; the way her breath was soft and steady in my ear. The lingering scent of cinnamon from her breakfast. The comforting weight of her body beside mine.

She was right. It was good to take in the little moments amongst all the chaos. Brookhaven might be small, but it was still big enough to bring danger to our door on an alarmingly frequent basis. And yet, I wouldn't have it any other way. I had no doubt that some mystery would befall our magical little town in the days and weeks to come. But for now, I could sit and appreciate that once again, we'd put things right for this family I'd found.

A QUICK AUTHOR'S NOTE

I'M NOT USUALLY A DISCOVERY WRITER. I GENERALLY know what's going to happen before I start writing and, especially with mysteries, who did it and their motive. This time around, that wasn't the case. I came into this book knowing that Rick was going to be the first suspect and that he'd tick all the boxes of motive, means and opportunity.

But beyond that, I hadn't actually sorted out who was going to be the killer, let alone that there would be two folks involved. But as I wrote and started to see where the story led me, I loved that I realized it was Tessa and Louis who both had their reasons to want our scheming ring master dead. And even more than that, I continued to uncover little bits of the puzzle as went along in Darcy's investigation. The locket Louis tried to sell Tyson? That just appeared in the moment and linked both him and Tessa to the crime. The torn up photograph? I didn't realize until after I'd written the scene in the trailer that it was the same one Darcy had discovered previously.

I have to say I really enjoyed this type of writing. Will it happen again? Could be. Part of me does hope it becomes a little bit more prevalent in my writing, although I am intending to work off more of an outline for Darcy's next adventure as we get to dig even more into Maggie's history and her family. One thing I really have enjoyed about crafting this longer series is the chances to really dive into the secondary characters and strengthen their links and relationships to Darcy.

Turn the page for a glimpse of High Roller...

HIGH ROLLER

Magic's a gamble...

Darcy can hardly believe it's been two years since she uprooted her life and settled in the supernatural town of Brookhaven. A full-fledged witch in her own right, she's delighted to have found her place in the world. Too bad her and Maggie's penchant for solving magical mysteries has made its way beyond the town's borders.

Just as Darcy and her friends are about to celebrate the anniversary of her arrival, an unexpected face from Maggie's past resurfaces. Her wayward brother has come looking for help with his sizable gambling debt. He begs for Maggie's help in rescuing his new wife and baby from the clutches of an online gambling syndicate.

Not willing to let her girlfriend fall back into dangerous habits, Darcy resolves to use whatever magic is necessary to find the kidnapping victims and free Maggie's family from the specter of the faceless goons. But the deeper Maggie goes into the world of online, high-stakes gambling, the more Darcy worries that all the magic in the world won't be enough to beat the house.

Scan the QR code to get High Roller

ABOUT THE AUTHOR

S.E. Biglow is the pen name of *USA Today* bestselling author Sarah Biglow. She lives in Massachusetts with her husband and son. She is a licensed attorney and spends her days combatting employment discrimination as an Investigator with the Mass-achusetts Commission Against Discrimination.

You can find an up-to-date list of all my books here